About the Author

Born and raised in Havana, Juan Carlos Wardito de Chivonez II came to Yorkshire, aged eight, in the early seventies when his family were deported for non-payment of sugar cane tax. Settling in Pudsey, where 't'ducks fly backward', he started writing punk poetry and then humorous Christmas messages to entertain his friends at work.

His classic line, "Your Xmas belly is full of grease, hers is full of turkey and that is never a good mix. Ask a Cypriot," still gets a laugh today.

The Three Amigos is his first novel.

The Three Amigos

Juan Carlos Wardito de Chivonez II

The Three Amigos

Olympia Publishers
London

www.olympiapublishers.com
OLYMPIA PAPERBACK EDITION

A CIP catalogue record for this title is
available from the British Library.

ISBN: 978-1-78830-835-9

First Published in 2020

Olympia Publishers
Tallis House
2 Tallis Street
London
EC4Y 0AB

Printed in Great Britain

Acknowledgements

There are so many people who have contributed to this book over the years in some form or another. You might not have even recognised yourselves in the story, which may be a good thing. To all of you, many thanks.

But I do want to mention a few special people.

First of all, the Selem family from Merida, who have been the kindest and most welcoming hosts, whilst I have sweated in the midday sun to write this bloody thing, offering me tacos and Tecate Light when I have hit a creative wall.

The PSC, without who my late forties and early fifties would not have been half as much fun, or as dangerous, and kept me interested in writing through their appreciation of my Xmas Message each year.

To Mick, for being my best friend and keeping me on the straight and straight.

To my kids, Young Condor and Ecuadorian Grey Eagle, or Jack and Cass which they prefer, who both encouraged me to come to Mexico, laugh at my shit jokes, find me Leeds United streams and offer tremendous support in all I do.

And my mum, who I hope never reads this, but has always been there every time that I have cocked up my life and there have been a few. I hope she appreciates poetic licence.

And finally, to the two other Amigos. Dave and Cornish

Mick, I know we haven't seen each other for years, but I hope you now see that all those long nights in the Junction Pub, Thornbury, were not totally without meaning.

Juan Carlos Wardito de Chivonez II

Introduction by the author

I believe it was the late, great roly-poly comedian Les Dawson who said that if you are going to write your one and only book, then you need to be in the right frame of mind and in the right place to do so.

To be honest, at the time of writing this, probably my one and only book, my mind was a bit messed up (I won't say fucked up in the introduction in case my mum ever reads this).

And renting a flat in Pontefract, the hallowed home of Haribo, which is fucking up the blood sugar counts of kids all over the world (sorry Mum), was not really helping.

Pontefract is to Yorkshire what Fred and Rose West were to parenting skills. A town full of bitter ex-miners, intent on lynching Margaret Thatcher even though she has been dead for years, although they don't even realise it yet because Jeremy Kyle never did a programme about it.

And dark pubs, full of big girls, in white leggings and high heels, singing their hearts out every Saturday night to some Celine Dion or Mariah Carey ballad before they blow off their tattooed Haribo packers for the price of a kebab and their Action Car home.

Yes, Uber has yet to reach Pontefract, as no one yet has a proper bank account, and the idea of not paying for a taxi with hard cash would be far too confusing to those who think A levels are one of the services on offer from that little whore in

Normanton.

But enough of slagging off Pontefract. I chose to live there so I am as much to blame as Margaret Thatcher for closing the pits and cutting off their only source of income and topical conversation.

Which leads me to the second reason for my fragile state of mind.

I had just been made redundant from my job as Head of Organisational Development, without any redundancy pay (thanks Luscious Lips), and was facing another few months searching for a job that I wouldn't want to do, definitely wouldn't pay enough and I would be lining into a younger boss with the people skills of a Russian shot putter.

Before I go on.

Head of Organisational Development. Sounds a bit wanky doesn't it?

Well it is.

Being the Head of O.D. means you just need to sound like you know about "culture", pretend you actually care about business performance and do a bit of management training, which everyone then ignores as soon as they get back to their day jobs.

But luckily, there are thousands of business leaders out there who believe their employees need to be highly motivated and engaged at work, even though most people just care about paying the mortgage, buying fags and their two weeks holiday in Fuerteventura, where they can forget about their shit jobs, slag off their bosses, buy cheap fags and get twatted on horrible cocktails that they would never normally drink at home.

But again, enough slagging off deluded business leaders, who "really want to make a difference to the lives of their people". I have done pretty well out of it, have had a few mortgages, smoked like a bastard chimney and did once spend two weeks in Fuerteventura but I only got sunstroke and crabs. But not necessarily in that order.

However, the thought of looking for another job was about as appealing as an orgy with the Spice Girls, where Baby Spice doesn't turn up and you have to make the choice between Ginger and Scary about which one sits on your face.

So apart from living in Ponte Carlo (they actually call it that, although the only similarity is that the French don't wash regularly either), and being made redundant without redundancy pay (thanks again Luscious Lips), why else was my head a shed?

Well, being a fifty-seven-year-old Cuban immigrant, divorced twice, with an ever balding head and an ever expanding stomach, a pension that was lost during the Matanzas sugar cane crop failure in '92; and with my son, Young Condor de Chivonez III, and my daughter, Ecuadorian Grey Eagle de Chivonez IV, both now living their own lives, I was at a bit of a crossroads in my mind. Well, to be totally honest, more of a spaghetti junction on acid.

So what could I do? What was I any good at?

After being made redundant (I hope Luscious Lips goes bust very quickly), I had watched all the decent box sets; the Sopranos, House of Lies, the Madcap Adventures of Merlin the Happy Pig in Menston and so now even TV was as boring as a Colin Jackson soliloquy on why British sprinters had once again failed at a major athletics championship.

If I had any decent morals, then I suppose I could have spent my free time doing voluntary work in one of the twenty thousand charity shops that line Pontefract's main High Street; SCOPE, the Heart Foundation, the Red Cross, Action against Thatcher, Save the Whale, Save the Snow Leopard, Save the Bolivian Pygmy Marmoset, the choice is endless.

However, the only one that held any real interest for me was Save the 1970s Comedians but that was closed down when Charlie Williams was massacred in broad daylight by Tom O'Connor during a racist joke-off in Blackpool. Being a black comedian in Barnsley in the 1970s was always going to be a tricky calling.

My reign as World Wanking Champion had ended during a pretty gruesome vasectomy in the early 90s, so that was never an option, especially now that the Chinese had entered the fray, and their Government imposed limit of two children per family meant they had millions of eager young men, ready with cock in hand.

I was never going to be a male gigolo. The average life expectancy of the male prostitute in the Pontefract region is less than that of the bomb disposal expert in Baghdad. There were countless stories, splashed all over the front page of the *Pontefract Observer*, of flattened carcasses being peeled from sticky mattresses in squalid bedsits where noble but hapless young men had made the fatal mistake of letting a fat lass from Ponte ride on top. Plus, the going rate was less than ten pounds per hour and that included buying them Malibu and a chicken korma.

The only real thing that I have ever been really interested in, or any good at, was writing.

I had learned to write at school, although I doubt such a profound revelation like that is going to win me the Nobel Prize for Literature. As a young boy, I had sat many a Matanzas evening on the knee of my Great Uncle Pedro de Chivonez VII, now a convicted paedophile, although he will always protest that he was just a bit over-friendly, listening to his wondrous tales of when Havana Club really tasted like Havana Club and when Fidel had defeated Che in the Cuban Bar Billiards league.

My love of stories and literature grew and I started the Juan Carlos Wardito Literary Club to bring together like-minded Cubans, although this proved to be a non-starter as most young and educated Cubans were simply into Samba dancing, mojitos and hating America. Even after being deported to England, I carried on writing a bit of poetry and prose, most of it for my own pleasure, but a few times for the amusement of my friends, Sir Ian Botham and the de Chivonez family.

As you have probably already gathered, I enjoy a good simile and the odd '70-'80s reference, but could I turn that very basic literary foundation into something as enthralling as *The Stud* by Jackie Collins or *Bravo Two Zero* by Andy McNab, which actually gets better after every read?

My great friend the gamekeeper, Seth Armstrong, once told me that to write the perfect book you had to be in the right place. And he should know after his seminal work "How to fight a ferret in a dustbin and come out on top", written under an Emmerdale full moon, knocked the Bible off top spot of the all-time best sellers list.

If you want to write a romantic novel, then you go to Paris.

If you want to write a historical drama, then you travel to Florence or Cairo. You want to tell the greatest ever adventure story, then you jump on the Trans-Siberian Express or get a bus to Halifax.

You don't believe me, then ask yourself: "Where did Thomas Harris go to create the serial killing monster Hannibal Lecter?"

Not New York, Moscow or Los Angeles, but Bradford, home to the Yorkshire Ripper, the Black Panther and Filthy Alice, who wasn't really a serial killer but a terrible and unhygienic cook, who took the lives of many a young Bradfordian with her sausage casserole and genital warts.

It is absolutely true that the most famous line in the *Silence of the Lambs*, and the subsequent film, had to be changed from the original 'I ate his liver with a chicken samosa, washed down with a nice mango lassi', simply to suit the American audience. My mum still tells tales of a small American man wandering around the streets of Manningham with a notebook, asking the locals if they carried a change of clothing and a small claw hammer.

But where could I go to write my masterpiece? Obviously, Pontefract was out, unless I wanted to write about small chewy sweets that lead to type two diabetes and ASBOs.

Cuba was definitely out. The whole de Chivonez family had been deported by Castro in the late '60s for tax evasion and rickets, becoming the first boat people to settle in the UK. Well, not really a boat but a barge on Rodley Canal, next to a lovely family from Cambodia called the Pol Pots, although they didn't stay long after a freak genocide of the local Thai boat people and the disappearance of my pet spaniel, Ramon.

And, even though he has been dead for twenty years, my father, the late Frederico de Chivonez I, still figures highly on Cuba's most wanted list, obviously after Batista but slightly ahead of Gloria Estefan. So, not Cuba.

Because of my slightly fragile mental state and recent redundancy, (this will be the last ever mention of Luscious Lips but your makeup is poor quality, overpriced and makes women look like cheap tarts), I wanted to feel tall among men again. Like Orson Welles in Citizen Kane, or like Gary Cooper in High Noon. But most of all, like Sean Bean in When Saturday Comes.

I wanted to stand out from the norm, be a talking point and, to be honest, feel a bit superior. I contemplated a few months with a tribe of pygmies in the Belgian Congo but found it didn't exist any more and that Bono had ballsed that up by buying all the pygmies platform shoes.

So I chose Merida, the state capital of the Yucatan Peninsula in Mexico, where the average height of the local Mayan is five foot six and, even at the age of fifty-seven, I reckon I could still fucking leather the lot of them.

And here I sit, outside a small hacienda in the district of Chiburna, sweating like Bernard Manning doing Tough Mudder, to write my book.

I first started messing with the idea for *The Three Amigos* about fifteen years ago but two marriages, a few years of absolute Dirty Sanchez madness with the greatest ever football firm, the Parka Service Crew, and a fondness for Creme Egg shooters meant it was never going to be properly written whilst I was in Yorkshire.

You might be disappointed if you are expecting a fabulous

adventure, or a passionate romance, or some political thriller that has you on the edge of your seat. However, I will muse philosophically like a young Peter Kay when he was still funny, make you squirm as if you are watching Naked Attraction with your mum and she asks you where have all the pubes gone, and take you to dark places that you believed only ever existed in Scotland.

Much of it will be true, although some of the dialogue will be made up as my memory is on a par with that of Shaun Ryder, but it is really up to you to decide on how deep your depraved mind wants to go. There is an order to these ramblings but no contents page, as I guess that you would all turn straight to the chapters on anal sex and Jimmy Floyd Hasselbaink. I know that I would.

This book is simply a take on life in '80s Bradford by Juan Carlos Wardito de Chivonez II.

Bon viveur, Cuban legend and once Head of O.D. for Luscious Lips. The cunts.

Fight

The Napier had never been as tense.

His hand trembled with anticipation, shaking the ash from his Embassy Number Ten all over the bar and forming a slurry lake with the half of mild that Tom from the bakery had spilt earlier.

"Go on you, old bastard" he thought, as Sid began his well-worn daily trek to the jukebox, ten pence in hand and ready to fill The Napier with *A Bat Out Of Hell*.

Barry was in quite a good mood today. Brenda, his slutwife and the peroxide queen of Bradford, was in Morecambe collecting lugworms for the annual fishing competition, the cat was dead and nobody had vomited in the toilets the night before.

He had been the landlord of The Napier for almost twenty years now and was proud that in all that time there had never been a fatality in the pub. There had been a birth, an attempted coup by Mongolian militia and a bucket load of stabbings, but never a death. Except the cat, who got locked in the jukebox and was only found when the maggots kept making the needle jump and repeating, *I'm in the Mood for Dancing* by the Nolans.

He readily admitted that the pub was in need of some modernisation and had only the previous day made enquiries about bringing in beef-flavoured crisps. It was a hell of a decision and he had sweated on it all night, before finally deciding to stick with ready salted and the occasional bag of cheese and onion at Christmas and on Benito Mussolini's birthday. The lads just weren't ready for it.

He remembered the time when he had been conned by the brewery into promoting a new German lager called Das Deutscher Piss. Everything was going fine until half past seven when the darts team set up a Stormtrooper unit and invaded Leeds, gassing the village idiot and building a new bypass around Bingley. Even Brenda had joined in by refusing to shave under her arms for a week. Barry knew change was dangerous.

During the seventies, he had worried about keeping up with fashion and had even gone as far as the Keegan perm. Unfortunately, having greasy blond hair meant that Barry spent 1977 looking like a twat with a very messy spaghetti carbonara on his head, and therefore had never fulfilled his sexual fantasy of fisting Nellie Pledge. Since then he hadn't bothered with his appearance and too many late nights, too much bitter and too little exercise had made him the big man that he was today. Fat, but happy.

Over the years Barry had often wondered why Sid has this fixation with Meatloaf.

Sid was well old. Meatloaf wasn't. Meatloaf is American. Sid was from Bradford but had been stationed in Catterick during the war and collared anyone he could to tell them about that time he had deloused his pubic hair with Blue Stratos. Meatloaf had loads of women. Sid had a wife called Mary who was dead, but he still slept with anyway, often inviting Tom from the bakery for a threesome.

The only thing that Barry thought they could possibly have in common was that five minutes of either was long enough. *A Bat Out Of Hell* made you feel like a satanic, sex-craved serial sodomiser, while five minutes of Sid left you craving any orifice into which to crawl and escape from his mange, bad breath and John Betjemen recitals.

Sid had now reached the dartboard and paused as one of the arrows sprang off the wire and blinded Tony's whippet, Helen Keller. Tony had been warned on plenty of occasions about letting the dog lick the taproom floor and now it was too late. A blind dog is no good to any man and people wept as Tony dragged Helen through the Snug towards her inevitable fate, Ram Jam's Curry Emporium. However, Barry, who had barred the whippet on several occasions for telling racist jokes and buggering the pub mascot, wasn't bothered.

He had been waiting all day for this moment and soon it was going to happen.

Barry first realised he had a sadistic streak during his teens when he tortured his mother by constantly playing *Puppy Love* on his radiogram and by always wearing Hi Karate aftershave. Although never bothering to have pets of his own, he initiated the Frog Whipping Post at the Blue Lagoon and had once shoved a banger up a cow's arse. Being a landlord had developed his skills further and provided plenty of opportunity to play out his sick mind games. But today was going to be the worst.

Being a pensioner, Sid didn't have much and he therefore thought wisely about spending his money. His diet consisted mainly of beans, dried fruit, Um Bongo and chips, and he kept warm in winter by burning bibles, given to him by a mad

Jehovah Witness from the Seaman's Mission next to Rodley Canal. He had always been mean, even during the heady days of the sixties when he refused to share LSD with his daughter, and made joss sticks by soaking bulrushes in Mary's Charlie Girl perfume.

But Sid always had money for two things. Five minutes of passion with the local prostitute and the coinage for *A Bat Out Of Hell*. Sid felt an affinity with Meatloaf, although he didn't really know why. And that is why he invested, yes invested, ten pence putting it on the jukebox every night for the last eight years. It was like going to church or being blown off by the local prostitute. A truly religious experience in the hallowed temple that was The Napier.

A bead of sweat dribbled off Barry's nose and onto the bar.

"Any minute now" he thought, his concentration focused solely on the aged sex machine making his way to the jukebox, ignoring the pleas for nuts and other bar snacks from a double glazing salesman, who just happened to have the misfortune to break down outside the worst pub in the world.

"Please, go on, it's just ten pence you, miserly old sod!" he mused.

Barry didn't really like Sid and wanted him to die. Over the years he had tried various methods of getting rid, including barring him for fighting, spitting, vomiting, fidgeting, necrophilia, fingering Brenda, smoking crack, spending too little, spending too much, being ugly, smelling, wearing a flat cap, going grey, fornicating, clicking his false teeth, breathing, dancing to Mud, farting, winning the 1980 darts and dominoes league, laughing, calling everybody "love", twitching, singing, moaning, staring at his pint, wearing overalls, being there, selling raffle tickets for the Baader-Meinhof gang, standing, sitting, squatting, lying down, lying, muckspreading, gossiping, origami, wrestling pigs, being drunk, being sober, getting on everyone's tits, gurning, soliciting, bestiality, vagrancy, turning the milk sour, earwax rolling, talking, chumping on Bonfire Night, slouching, not having a dog licence and putting *A Bat Out Of Hell* on the fucking jukebox every night.

But tonight would be different. There would be no backing down and the usual acceptance of Sid back into the pub after localised rioting, national press campaigns and a personal heartstrings letter from Betty Turpin, accepting full responsibility for all Sid's actions over the years. Barry knew that Sid's heart was in trouble. Seventy years of lard and mild, coupled with one Carry On film too many had left Sid on the edge. He was about to topple over and Barry was ready to push.

Sid paused at the jukebox to admire a curry stain on the wall, which was shaped exactly like the Inter-City Fairs Cup. He would mention that at tomorrow's Women's Institute meeting and get a laugh. His hand moved automatically to button D6, as his ten pence slid smoothly into the slot.

Barry began to giggle inanely, bits of tobacco tumbling from his nicotine stained teeth like badger dandruff. He knew it was time. Sid would die. He must. His heart wouldn't be able to stand it. Eight years was too long. The shock would...

"Well I'll be buggered," mumbled Sid to himself, as he always did, being a sad, pathetic old man, "I've been coming here for nigh on forty years and I've never seen that before".

His hand slowly moved away from D6 and towards F10, *The Lord's Prayer* by Mario Lanza. It was the song to which Mary and he had first whisked milk and made pancakes to all those years ago, and he still missed her golden syrup soaked pinny today.

Barry's mouth fell open as the first few bars echoed around the pub. He had not felt so numb since drinking meths in the local graveyard and going into quite a serious coma. He had been planning for this moment for two years.

The idea had first come to him while watching Brenda file her toenails, as she did every Tuesday, with a rasp the size of a small dolphin. He realised that he hated certain things about his life and decided to do something about it.

Nothing major of course, such as dieting, exercising or being nice to his customers. But little things, like buying Brenda some knickers that weren't the size of tablecloths and the colour of eggshells, combing his hair slightly differently on games nights, giving up his Chaos Theory night classes which were far too easy for him and, of course, killing Sid.

That morning, even before the cavity wall insulation salesman had been, Barry had got up, gone down to the bar and switched D6. Sid was sure to put it on tonight and, with the small doses of iron filings and beetle shit that Barry had been putting in his beer for the last fortnight, the shock of *Jilted John* by Jilted John instead of *A Bat Out Of Hell* would definitely send Sid over the edge.

Fortunately for Sid, he had trapped a pube in his braces as he bent to put on the record, and was therefore was not standing up to receive the jet-propelled ashtray in his face.

"You fucking old bastard!" screamed Barry as he ripped

the sheet of pork scratchings off the wall and started to hurl them at the cowering OAP. Sweat popped out of his forehead and his eyes bulged like bulls' testicles. He had really lost it.

"Twenty bleeding years of you whining about the beer! Twenty bleeding years of watching you smirk that smug fucking grin when you pick up double blank you bastard! Twenty bleeding years of watching you constantly snook up that dribble of snot from your Brain Clough nose!"

He had now run out of scratchings and had started to throw packets of scampi fries.

"I hate you and plan for you to die, and then like the complete bastard that you are, and probably all your ancestors have ever been, after twenty bleeding years of musical banality, you suddenly develop an appetite for classical Italian tenors!"

The fries had now gone and glasses began to arc towards Sid, who completely mystified by the sudden outburst, stood by the jukebox furiously stuffing the packs of assorted snacks into his donkey jacket.

"You will die," his face now the colour of a baboon's arse and just as ugly.

"Desist this at once Landlord. Sidney is a valued elder of the community, who unfortunately has a distorted vision of reality and an ambivalent view of society's expectations." Tommy laid his hand on Barry's arm to stop the onslaught of glasses. Tommy had once read a book.

"Piss off Tommy," said Barry as he punched the learned scholar's face leaving an imprint of his half sovereign ring on Tommy's cheek and some fingernail slime on his chin.

"Fuck You Barry" said a man, who had never been in the

pub before, but saw it as an ideal opportunity to get into this book, as he jumped over the bar and began to pummel Barry's expanse of midriff but without much success.

Within forty seconds of the song beginning, the whole pub had joined in the fight. Gladiators arrived from everywhere. The taproom, the snug, the David Hockney lounge. Even Barry's bit on the side, Doreen "Banana Breasts" Dean had left her Angling Today and was currently kicking the head in of Shirley, cake shop owner and slag, Spencer. Tony's blind dog Helen made a brief reappearance but got confused after bumping into the pool table five times and trying to bite the fire extinguisher. The bar was awash with blood, mild and traces of Sanatogen from the older warriors. Someone had really got into the mood and put *Kung Fu Fighting* by Carl Douglas on the jukebox, leading to a roundhouse kick to Sid's ribcage and some quite serious chafing.

The only people not fighting were The Three Amigos at the corner table in The Green Room. They were in some sort of trance, completely oblivious to the blood and stomach pills around them.

Hey Ho, Let's Go

Joey was on top form, slurring his way through *Sheena is a Punk Rocker* before Dee Dee counted him into *Teenage Lobotomy*, his gravelly voice pushing the fifty thousand crowd in Bradford Moor Park towards a mad, pogoing frenzy matched only by the bounce in Rachel Welch's tits.

The Ramones in a free open-air concert on Bradford Moor! A Berlin Wall of Marshall speakers set up next to the boating lake, just in front of the swings. They had been playing for nearly seven hours and still not one of their songs had sounded the same or been separated by a two second gap.

The sun was out and the air was warm, encouraging the forty-nine thousand, nine hundred and ninety-seven other crowd members to loosen their school ties and blouses, hitch up their black, woollen knee-length stockings and remove their brilliant white panties. However, everything and everybody was cool as ice cold Skol lager spewed forth from dozens of geysers placed around the park and peace was ensured by the Laisterdyke Hells Angels chapter, the Suzuki FS80s.

Obviously, The Three Amigos had the best backstage passes available. Although later they would be stage diving into the ocean of nubile minge, with a cast iron guarantee of pre-pubescent sex, at the moment they were sharing a cheese football and Double Diamond buffet with Led Zeppelin in a clear perspex VIP area at the side of the stage. Zeppelin had provided the support, along with David Bowie in his Ziggy Stardust era, the Clash, Althea and Donna, U2 only doing the songs from *Boy,* and Debbie Harry, naked and with whipped cream spread all over her smooth, delicious thighs.

It had pissed on Live Aid and, although no money had been collected and no crops of turnips would be springing up in Tanzania, the boys knew that a sense of love, peace and red-hot sex would be emanating from Bradford tonight.

A massive joint was being passed around the group, rolled one-handed by John Bonham as he fingered a Dutch groupie, stuffed with the finest ganja this side of Pudsey and providing a smoke as cool as Chris Waddle's mullet. Unlike the normal blow, this didn't make you tired and want to eat the world's supply of Star Bars before you passed out in front of *Charlie's Angels*, trousers around your ankles. This gear made you speak intelligently and philosophise wisely on life like a young Ken Barlow.

Somewhere in the background, Billy, Mark and Danny, The Three Amigos in question, heard the Barker Boys getting a real good kicking from the kids of Bradford Moor Primary School. It was about time. The Barker Boys, Garry and Larry, made it their aim in life to stop everybody's fun, even stealing dibbers and dabbers from grannies on their way to the bingo. But now, as Garry ran through the backstage area with a pencil in the back of his head and a ruler stuck up his arse, the boys knew that not even they could spoil the day.

"So boys, do you fancy coming on tour with me to Japan in May?" Kate Bush had just walked into the VIP area. Although she hadn't been asked to play because her music was so fucking awful, the boys had asked her along for novelty value. "I am afraid there won't be much room on the tour bus, so you will all have to share a bunk with me."

Billy took a big drag on the joint before passing it to Jimmy Page. "Sorry Kate. As much as we love to share your bunk, in May we are all acting as personal dressers and fuck buddies to Chrissie Hynde on her world tour."

"So you can go now," added Danny, waving a dismissive hand in the direction of the Wuthering Heights star and, although she had been a stalwart of the British Music industry for nearly a decade, the poor bitch left in tears.

"That was a bit harsh," said Mark, who was always the sensitive one. But then, a six-foot Norwegian porn star, wearing nothing but a pair of Parsley the Lion panties ground her way into his lap and he soon forgot about Kate Bush or Kate or any Bush apart from the one gyrating against him.

"Do you want an encore Boys?" shouted Joey Ramone from the edge of the stage. "Only Johnny's fingers are starting to bleed quite fucking badly!"

"Just give us *Rockaway Beach* one more time and we will call it a night." replied Danny. "I have to be at work for seven and we still have some serious shagging to do."

"And I have an exam in the morning, although I already know that I will pass" added Billy, rolling another spliff.

"Yeah and I have a big delivery of haddock coming from Cleethorpes" said Mark, as the Norwegian beauty guided him towards the twenty foot water bed in the corner.

And so, as the sun gradually faded over the Bradford skyline, the boys indulged themselves in an orgy of sex, drugs and rock and roll, the like of which had never been seen on a West Yorkshire ordnance survey map since Caligula first opened Bramley Baths by filling it full of piss.

Animal

Billy knew his dad was still up the moment he turned into his drive and heard that same gang of ruthless crocodiles ripping zebras, impalas and springboks apart in the living room. He silently opened the back door and slipped into the kitchen, hoping to get upstairs and into bed without disturbing the old man.

He wasn't in the mood for him. It had been a good night and his head was still buzzing from the sounds and pictures that the three of them had created.

His dad was getting to be more and more like the animals he constantly watched on the television. At times he was inanimate like the great bull seal, yet his eyes scanned the screen, as would an eagle searching for arctic hares. His hunched-up frame resembled that of a praying mantis and his skin was becoming tough like a warthog's scrotum.

Billy was starting to get worried. Was this condition hereditary? His granddad, exiled from Cuba in the '50s, had gone the same way. Believing himself to be a llama, he had spent his last years wandering around Bradford dressed in colourful blanket wear, chewing coca leaves and spitting at people. It had finally come to an end when a gay Gaucho from Grimsby rounded him up and took him on a Wild West tour of Humberside, where he was killed for his pelt.

Billy once had a hamster, who had died after snorting

Airfix kit glue and tightrope walking across the washing line. But Billy wasn't fat, his eyes didn't pop out if you held him upside (or did they?) and he didn't cram food into his cheeks, apart from Mars Bars, which were his favourite. His hair was a sandy brown, very much like Hammy the Glorious Rodent, and he had once tried eating hamster food for a bet, but it hadn't affected his life or given him a craving for cheese.

But his dad was going seriously mental.

"Is that you Billy?" Billy stopped at the bottom of the stairs and swore at the picture of David Cassidy that hung above the cloakroom cupboard.

"Yes Dad. Do you want a cup of tea?" Billy knew what the answer would be.

"Only if you're making one son". He moved back into the kitchen and filled up the kettle from the tap. He knew that his dad would have been sat there since he had left at seven and that he would be sat there for another five hours.

In fact, his dad had been sat there for ten years and hadn't made so much as a Baked Alaska or Tournedos Rossini since Billy's mum had gone in '76. She had finally left during an extremely graphic programme on the reproductive cycle of the Canadian woodlouse, which his dad had been silently masturbating to in the lounge. She had put up with a range of his wild habits over the years. Never complaining when he brought home dead mice or birds, or when he marked out his territory by pissing on the couch, she had finally packed her bags when he had started coughing up furballs in bed and grooming her pubic hair for ticks.

It had been a difficult time for Billy, who was fifteen and just starting to ask questions about the right consistency of pastry for a successful fruit flan, how to knit a Leeds United scarf and the best method for making the girls at school squirt. However, his dad had not even noticed that she had gone or mentioned her since.

Billy knew that his dad was insane but he was happy, and it would have been quite ironic to have him locked up in a padded cell when all he did was watch animals freely roaming around their natural habitat.

"Thanks son." He didn't even glance up as Billy placed the mug of tea beside him, along with a full plate of cheese sandwiches. The empty plate from the sausage and egg tea, which Billy had made before leaving, was still by the side of the TV, alongside a pile of cashew nut shells. Obviously, he had been watching a programme about Amazonian howler monkeys. Billy sat down on the threadbare couch, pitted with holes from his wild cat clawing, and watched his dad.

He knew that one day he would have to leave him, like an ocelot abandons her kittens, but realised that the chances of him coping on his own were slim. He had learned to wash himself, could suckle on a bottle of stout, but in the dog eat dog world that was looking after yourself, Billy's dad had as much chance of surviving as a Man U fan in Leeds.

And that day would be sooner than later. Billy had nearly finished his Spanish degree and would one day be taking up a post teaching English to Spanish whores in a Bilbao brothel. His finals were due in a couple of months and he had just started his revision, which was difficult enough without having to look after his dad.

Being of Cuban descent, Spanish was always part of his life but it really began at the age of eight while watching the

1970 Brazilian football team win the World Cup in Mexico. For a lad brought up on damp grass and playground concrete, the idea of having a kickabout on warm sand everyday was simply fantastic. He adopted the Brazilian style to his own game and became known at Bolton Royd Primary School as the Pinkish Jairzinho, covering himself on more than one occasion with gravy browning, although he already had olive skin, and adapting a Samba dance to *Cum on feel the Noize* by Slade.

As he became older, his desire to go and live in Brazil was fuelled by pictures of thonged, latino beauties and more kickabouts on the beach. At school he had seen the film "Tess" and Angel Claire, the wanker who doesn't give Nastassja Kinski one, went to Brazil. At the age of thirteen, Billy applied for Brazilian citizenship after writing to the embassy in Liverpool. He had now changed his name to Juan Carlos Wardito and, along with his best mate Luis Alfonso Fraserino, alias Graham Gaunt (skinny kid who once pissed himself in assembly), they eagerly awaited the decision.

They were devastated when their application for citizenship was turned down due to their age, their crap hairstyles and the fact that they couldn't speak the language. The next day at school, Billy dropped Astral Physics and began Spanish lessons with Senorita Jones, who was from Wales but had once been on a package tour to Lloret de Mar. She had the lot. The Catalan accent, the way of saying "thhhh" instead of using "c" in "Barthelona" and the colourful, stuffed donkey with the eyes that came out and blinded infants. He was enchanted with her tapas and the coal dust that sprinkled from her nose when she gave head to Senor Barnett, the history teacher, behind the science lab. It was the first time that Billy had really felt in love and he concentrated solely on his studies.

This became much easier when Luis Alfonso dropped the classes. He kept trying to wind Billy up by telling him that they spoke Portuguese in Brazil and that he was shit at football anyway. Luis had fallen in love with a Ukrainian princess in 5C and began studying O' levels in queuing, making wholesome meals from mouldy, old lettuce leaves and hating Russia.

Over the years his grasp of the language had developed. There had been the polecat spotting tour of Torremolinos when Billy was fifteen and just developing a taste for Pernod and punk rock. He vividly remembered all three of them being stopped at the departure gate in the airport for carrying metal objects. His dad had a polecat tagging device, mum had her nipples pierced and he had a "Mummy What Is A Sex Pistol?" badge hidden in his underpants so as not to appear subversive to the Spanish fascists that he was sure to encounter.

It was difficult being a teenage punk in Spain. Spitting sangria and pogoing to Flamenco was not really accepted and Billy spent most of the holiday watching French *Emmanuelle* films with Spanish subtitles. Not only did this improve his legendary lovemaking technique but it also boosted his Spanish vocabulary, especially in important areas such as ordering room service in a Bangkok hotel, hiring an open-top car and going down on foreign birds. Never afraid of a challenge, he had tried this out with the young Spanish maid at the hotel but had ended up with a ham roll and herpes.

Brenda, the landlady of The Napier, had also shown an interest in his linguistic diversity. She believed in all things

Latino, having once got pissed on tequila and bought *Begin The Beguine* by Julio Iglesias, and was therefore very impressed when one of her pool team called her Senorita when ordering his pie and peas supper.

So impressed that she offered him oral sex in the cellar after Barry had gone to bed. Billy was shit at pool but he had never had oral sex, unless you count the time when he had shoved his dick in the Hoover. Therefore, he hung about until all the others were gone, until it was just he and Brenda and the smell of pork scratchings and chalk.

Although he didn't go to the dentist every six months, Billy's teeth were still fairly white but not as white as Brenda's as she popped them in a half pint glass of mild, next to the Guinness barrel.

"Speak Spanish to me, my little Don Kwixot" mumbled Brenda, as her gums closed around him like a carp sucking gobstoppers. Billy however, had gone completely blank and where he should have been muttering sweet Latino nothings to his new friend, he could only remember the names of the 1978 Argentinean World Cup winning side.

"Passerella, Tarantini" and Brenda groaned with obvious pleasure.

"Ardiles, Villa" and Billy groaned with both pleasure and pain as Brenda became a demented beaver, gnawing away at the bark on his tree trunk.

"Kempes, Luceeeeeeeee!!" as he succumbed to the most natural instinct in the world.

Billy was not proud about what he had done. In fact, he had avoided Brenda and rice pudding for a couple of weeks after that and his stomach still heaved each morning as he squeezed the toothpaste tube. However, he continued with his Spanish, completely fluked his A Levels by doing them pissed up on cider and black and was now in his final year at Bradford University.

"Good night dad." "Good night son."

His dad had begun regurgitating his sandwiches in preparation for the feeding of the imaginary brood of Andean condors that he kept in the pantry, and therefore Billy decided it was time to go to bed. He went into his room, picked up his guide to Spanish sherry distilleries and began to read.

It had been brilliant tonight and he began to think about what would happen to the others when it was time for him to leave. They had been together so long that Billy couldn't imagine moving away. He looked at the clock, saw that it was nearing midnight and put on his headphones. It was a full moon and his dad would soon start baying, trying to attract a she-wolf that he could mate with before the rainy season began.

Pixie

Mark was still laughing to himself as he chopped up the onion and tossed it into the frying pan. It had been a brilliant night and even Billy had taken time off from his revision, which helped to make the pictures more vivid. It made life more bearable.

A little dash of Tabasco, some leftover fried rice, a touch of paprika, a handful of frozen peas and Mark had a rice supper fit for a Plymouth Argyle fan. He had learnt to cook during his time at sea and it had come in very useful since marrying the fat arsed lazy cow, who was now asleep on the sofa in front of him, a can of Hofmeister and a plate of chips decorating the carpet. The whole range of her culinary talent on display. Although he loved her in a strange kind of way, he often found himself reminiscing about his youth and wondering how he had ended up in a hopeless marriage in a northern town.

He was born in Cornwall in 1960, the bastard son of a pixie, who had raped a creamy nymphomaniac serving wench in a Cornish custard factory. Brought up by his Grandma Frank on an apple farm in Dorset, Mark had spent most of his childhood in a cidric daze, often only venturing out of the house to feed The Great Hound, and kill rabbits on St Austell's day. Most of his time was spent reading Famous Five books, especially the ones where the children went camping together and smoked crack. Mark liked George, the transsexual one, because she seemed to have the best of both worlds. Climbing trees with Dick and Julian and lesbian romps with Anne.

He had a difficult time at school, which is pretty typical for children brought up in a county where talking slowly and stupidly are a measure of intelligence. Although his dad lived with the Great Golden Dwarf of Penzance, and wasn't really a pixie but a short man with a fairy fixation, he would often turn up on parent's evenings in pointy shoes, a bell on his head and pretend to turn all the teachers into frogs. Mark's mum, who had split up with the pixie and become a working-class hooker in a Dorset Pig Factory, was also a bit embarrassing, getting gangbanged by the fourth form for the price of a clotted cream scone.

The teachers never really understood Mark and often made him stand outside the classroom for the whole term. Mr Spark, the religious flagellation teacher, who often whipped boys with liquorice bootlaces for simply masturbating in class, took a real dislike to him. Not content with ridiculing Grandma Frank by forcing her to recite Pam Ayres poems in class, he once nailed Mark to the blackboard for reciting the lyrics of *I Love to Love* by Tina Charles in the third form petting zoo.

Mark had left school at fourteen, which is about the legal age for pony baiting in Cornwall, and had fled to the sea. Well, when I say fled, I really mean led. A homosexual halibut fisherman called Captain Arthur Penworthy, who kept chinchillas and lizards, had whisked him away to sea as part of his sad wretch crew. This crew was made up from a range of adolescent misfits and freaks from right across the south of England. There was a boy with a clubfoot from Shrewsbury, a girl with no nipples from Bournemouth and the one intelligent teenager from Poole, as well as the whole of the Portland Bill Boys Brigade band.

The ship, the Jiggery Pokery, sailed out far into the Atlantic for years on end, searching for the legendary Giant Sea Squid of Rabobank, which Captain Penworthy believed to have magical powers that not only cured gout but also removed stubborn lipstick stains from neglected foreskins. It was a crusty old schooner but Captain Penworthy was proud of it, loved it and bathed it in Dettol every morning.

The crew was a happy bunch of young, pubescent misfits and Mark, for the first time in his life, felt comfortable among people of his own age. He enjoyed the early mornings, the fresh air, and the sound of seabirds screeching as Captain Penworthy harpooned them, stuffed them with anchovies and fed them to the ship's panther. He made a special friend of Katie, a freckled sixteen-year-old from Brighton, who was on the run from the Secret Police for being too ugly, a common enough crime in Sussex.

Their love flourished, and despite Captain Penworthy's homosexual advances on Mark, he proposed to her on his sixteenth birthday.

"Will you take my hand in marriage, you Southern Belle?" he asked, lovingly caressing the loose flap of skin that covered her hump.

"I will my fishy treasure" Katie replied, tears exploding from her eye, as she lovingly cooked him Kedgeree with a Coco Pop frosting.

They became inseparable, even washing together as the ship plundered the sardine and fishcake fields of Southern Spain. Mark also withdrew from the weekly skate shagging competitions, which were an integral part of man's induction into the squalid world of deep-sea fishing, and meant that he could no longer take the ship's ration. A tot of rum, a dried biscuit and anal sex with the ship's cat.

The date was set for the wedding. The seventeenth of October in the Year of Our Lord 1976. Mark pawned his 1970 Esso World Cup Coin Collection to buy a thirty-four-carat gold wedding band from a Toledo jewellery bandit and Katie brushed her teeth so that she could kiss her husband after the ceremony without giving him cold sores and warts. Captain Penworthy, as was his right as captain of the vessel, performed the ceremony, as two southern misfits became one under a soulful Mediterranean sunset.

The celebrations went on late into the night, with the revellers becoming more and more boisterous as they feasted on Cod in a White Wine Sauce and copious amounts of Cinzano Bianco and Pils Snakebite.

Very soon the party began to take a more sinister, sexual twist. The ship's cat exploded from overindulgence, Captain Penworthy passed out from sucking too much cock, and so the attention of the miscreants turned to the blushing bride. Mark could sense that something dreadful was about to happen and made plans to abandon the ship. He released the ropes to the small dinghy that acted as the ship's lifeboat, threw in some Wagon Wheels and prepared to get Katie.

He ran down into the galley to fetch his new bride but, to his horror, discovered that Danny Goon, the Action Man thief from Trowbridge, had got there before him. Spread-eagled on the galley table, his lovely wife was being pounded by a man with gripping hands and realistic hair, and she was enjoying it.

Her eye was gleaming, as she groaned with pleasure, seemingly to encourage George Moor, the boy who brought the Stylophone to Totnes, to take over when Danny was spent.

Mark turned away and retched. Although he had felt pain when his father abandoned him in favour of searching for Princess Paula, the Pregnant Postmistress from Plymouth, he had never experienced hurt this deep. Leaving the galley and his lovely wife, he took his few belongings, jumped into the dinghy and cast himself adrift on the blue expanse of the Mediterranean. He never wanted to see Katie or the Jiggery Pokery again.

He spent the next few days drifting aimlessly and reciting scripts from *Love Thy Neighbour*, which was Katie's personal favourite. Days turned into weeks, the sun constantly baking down with no sign of land. Mark developed an incredible thirst and very soon began drinking his own urine. Not that he had to, but simply because he was fed up with the cans of Double Diamond that he had brought with him and fancied a change.

It was three months later when, washed ashore on a Bridlington beach with an assortment of contraceptives and Bay City Roller albums, he first arrived in Yorkshire. Straightaway he seemed to find some affinity with the place. People did not question his strange accent or comment on his wanky haircut. Nobody looked down on him for using his knife to eat his peas and talking about pixies.

He found a job gutting mackerel in the local fish market, working and saving hard. The money was not great but life was simple and he kept his outgoings to a minimum by sleeping in the fish freezer and eating whelks. Mark made some friends among his fellow fishgutters, rekindled his relationship with skate during Christmas parties and birthdays, and slowly began to forget all about that treacherous bitch Katie and his time at sea.

Amanda, his wife, rolled over in her sleep and her copious stomach tumbled out of her black leggings and onto the top of her chips, covering her belly with Chop Sauce. Wiping the bead of snot away from her nose, he tidied away her can and plate. Best leave her to sleep on the floor rather than wake her and have another row. They were expecting a delivery of haddock for the Fish and Chip shop in the morning and it looked like Mark would be the one who was getting up. Billy and Danny helped but, although it was Bradford 1986, he was back in Dorset and wishing his life away.

Sage

Danny zipped up his leather jacket really tight, as he stepped out into the freezing, November night and cursed Bradford. He had been in a brilliant mood when he got in from the pub and now, he would get cold. The three of them had been in top form and not even a mass pub brawl had interfered with their pictures. However, it was now just past midnight and Brandy had been nagging him for the last twenty minutes for a walk. He knew that resistance was useless unless he wanted a big, yellow puddle on the kitchen floor.

He crossed the street and headed towards the small patch of woodland that hid between the bakery and the golf course. Brandy thought that rabbits lived there, although any semblance of wildlife had long since disappeared from this particular part of Bradford. Anyway, she would be quite happy chasing shadows while Danny chatted with H. It had been a while since they had last spoken, as Harry had been travelling throughout Asia for the last five months, spreading his message to the people of India and China. But Danny somehow knew that he would be there tonight. And he was right.

A small fire lit up the copse and, in the glow that emanated, Danny recognised the crinkly, grey hair and the broad grin as he approached. The customary pile of empty wine bottles was there, as well as a stack of books and magazines. H reached for a glass as Danny let Brandy off the leash and sat down beside him.

"Would Sir like a glass of the Mouton Cadet '83 or would he prefer a can of the finest Danish lager?"

"Wine at this time of night would surely interfere with one's digestion, would it not? Lager will suffice."

"A wise choice young Sir," H reached for a can of Heineken but passed the empty glass to Danny, "but decorum still insists on a glass." Danny smiled, used to the ritual but never bored or irritated by it, and poured the lager into the crystal cut goblet. He looked at the small, hunched figure before him. He seemed to have aged quite a lot over the last few months. The lines around his eyes and on his forehead looked deeper and darker, although that may have had something to do with his suntan, and his clothes looked definitely more lived in than when he had last spoken to him in February.

"So what brings you back to these parts?" asked Danny.

"Two things." H reached for the packet of King Edward cigars from his jacket, took one out and lit it up. "The first is to see the family. My daughter Sandra has decided to get engaged and I need to be sure that he is right for her." H paused as he gazed into the fire.

"And the other thing?" asked Danny.

"And the other thing, young Sir, is you. A little bird from across the water tells me that you are getting into trouble again."

Danny looked away. He had known H all of his life and yet one look, or one quiet word, could still make him feel like a ten-year-old. Harry had always been there, ever since Danny could remember. At Christmas, birthday parties, weddings and the like. He had been best friends with Danny's dad, had looked after his mum when his dad died and taken Danny's brother Alan under his wing, when he was caught and prosecuted for smuggling Samson contraband rolling baccy, crates of Grolsch and Israeli combat trousers into the local parachute regiment. He had also helped Danny and all the other lads on numerous occasions, especially Billy when his mum had left. He had lent them money, provided a room when things were bad at home and, in Danny's case, bailed him out of trouble with the police.

He knew who the little bird was. Alan, one-time best friend and brother, who was now a "respectable" double glazing salesman and lived in Yeadon, a town well known for its airport and tarn. It was Alan, who had collected him from the police station and tried to lecture him about right and wrong. Just a little hypocritical for someone who, in order, had been in trouble for the following:

Truancy

Stealing Curly Wurlys from Mr Singh, the newsagent

Demanding money with menace (nicking dinner money off first formers)

Setting off bangers during assembly

Sent home from school for fighting

Suspended from school for fighting

Expelled from school for running over the school mascot, a pregnant mongoose, on his Chopper and then kicking the shit out of the Headmaster

Arrested for urinating in a public place (The ABC cinema during *Grease*)

Running a tobacco and alcohol trafficking operation (cheap Samson tobacco and Grolsch)

Bestiality (only kidding but he once stroked a cat in a little bit too friendly kind of way)

Selling Israeli combat trousers and genuine bandoleers so that half of Laisterdyke appeared as if they were at war. Which they usually were anyway.

Being the porn king of Bradford. Well he owned twenty-three Jazz mags and a cine film from Copenhagen

Fighting Man U fans (unlucky to be caught for that one)

And finally, sleeping with Brenda, the landlady from The Napier. Not actually arrested but should have been.

Danny cared a lot about Alan but thought he was an arsehole. Getting expelled from school, marrying the first girl who had shown any real interest in him, even when he had won a load of cash, getting her pregnant and moving to fucking Yeadon. Top role model.

"So what was it this time? A protest against the collective works of David Hockney or the resurgence of the 'Bradford is Crap' campaign?" H tapped the ash from his cigar into the fire. Danny grinned, took a swig from his lager and lit a Regal King size.

"Making Kung Fu death stars at work and selling them to the Inter City Service Crew. You know that I like to put my creative talents to good use."

"Yeah but Kung Fu death stars went out in the seventies. Where's your contemporary vision young Sir?" H was hardly able to keep himself from laughing, although he realised the seriousness of what Danny had done. Over the years he had become used to his excursions into rebelliousness but noticed that, in recent times, these had taken on more of a sinister edge. "So how come you were caught? Not normally like the Young Danny to be so careless."

"One got lodged in a Policeman's helmet at the recent Chelsea game. I presume they examined it, saw it was marked with *Made by Danny McDonald, Radebe Engineering, Bradford*, put two and two together and came after me."

"And...?"

"And I got a two-year suspended sentence from the courts and a final written warning from work." Danny threw the cigarette into the fire and leant back to face H. "So am I stupid or what?" His voice had changed. Gone was any trace of joviality.

"What do you want me to say Danny? Yes, you are stupid and I think it's about time that you stopped all this pissing about. Or no, it was a brilliant idea, I admire your creative talent, the fact is that you are a one-man walking time-bomb and will probably end up out on the street or in prison. All I want to know is why?"

Danny knew why. It was all around him. Every time he woke up in the morning and looked out of the window. The row upon row of dark terraces. The squally black rain, which made everything and everybody appear damp and dirty. The fucking cats meowing every night outside his bedroom window. The monotonous, wet journey to the works, the same bored faces at work all hating the same thing every day. The even more tedious journey back in the rain and dodging the traffic, Blockbusters and then bed.

He was twenty-three years old. He had been in the works since he left school at sixteen and nothing had changed. He had the same boss. The same workmates who, although as pissed off as he was, still had their stupid little plastic snap boxes, bought *The Sun* and talked about the girls they had never shagged over the weekend. He still had the same mug for his tea that he used at sixteen. Even the rats were the same and, since he completed his apprenticeship, had started to call him by his first name as they now felt he was worthy of their presence.

"Why don't you come with me? I am going on a promotional tour of Egypt in a few weeks and need an assistant to carry my wine and books."

Danny knew what H was trying to do. By getting him out of Bradford, H was hoping that he would keep out of trouble but Danny knew that it wasn't a good enough reason to leave.

"Yeah, and what would you do when I killed a camel or headbutted an Arab? H, you know that I have to see this through myself. If I just leave, then I will drift back. When I go, it will be because I really, really see a purpose for leaving and I know that I will never come back."

H emptied the bottle and placed it gently among the others. "Well, be careful and stick close to Billy and Mark. Listen to Mark. He may be a slightly camp Cornish fisherman but he knows what is right. You aren't a bad lad. Just a sodding daft sense of humour and a twisted sense of irony."

"A typical Yorkshire bloke, right?" asked Danny as he threw his can on the fire and smiled at the old man.

"Right, but with a touch of a Celtic passion which makes you different to most of the twats around here. Look after yourself and I'll see you soon". H climbed into his sleeping bag and settled down.

Danny whistled and Brandy came running, a huge pair of white, cotton knickers in her mouth, and shot off towards the house. Not normally like her to be in such a rush to get home. And then, almost as quickly, Danny realised why. The tree branches parted and a naked Wendy Does Wyke burst into the copse, immediately doubling the amount of foliage on view. "Bradford does have its own wildlife," thought Danny, as the sixteen stone temptress attempted to appear coy by covering her own bush with another one.

"Where's your fucking dog?" she barked almost poetically. Danny turned and started to walk away. He had seen it all before and anyway, he was due at work in three hours and didn't want nightmares.

Party

The Napier had never been more festive.

It was New Year's Eve and the pub was packed. The Three Amigos, sat in their customary seats in the Green Room, were rocking on a mixture of Tetley's bitter, speed and Brenda's party fare, including tuna baps and Spam quiche, her speciality. They had been in since five but it had taken them a while to get into the spirit of the evening, especially as Mark had a massive row with wife and cow Amanda about the size of their haddock portions and mushy pea consistency.

It was now ten o'clock and the pub had just enjoyed a performance by Bradford Girls School Sixth-Form Naked Gymnastic Display team, with strategically placed minicams on certain apparatus, such as the beam and horse. Barry, in his role as Master of Ceremonies for the evening, had provided a very graphic but tasteful commentary to the proceeding and, surprisingly had not said "fanny" once.

Adopting the Barry Davies technique of understatement but enthusiasm, he hadn't flinched even when one of the girls had stretched a little too much and popped a stitch left in from her teenage pregnancy, or when another girl slipped over Sid's bottle of Barley Wine and made it disappear. The boys were thrilled with the routines and also the quality of the camera shots, which were able to distinguish between sixteen different shades of pink. In fact, the young ladies had gone down a treat and were now certain to receive the funding they required to get them to the 1988 Naked Gymnastic Olympics. Through sales of their video, souvenir blowjobs and the fact that Sid had signed over his pension for the next twenty years for the price of a personal floor exercise.

This was just part of the splendid evening's entertainment that Barry had organised.

He had toyed with a number of ideas to make the evening memorable, writing to both Delia Smith and Peter Stringfellow, for tips on choux pastry and how to set up a lap dancing lounge in the Snug. The Blindfold Darts competition had been a great success, although it was tinged with a little sadness. Tony, who had won after scoring a double Sid's temple, was then persuaded into giving an exhibition match with Brian Dibble, the kinky wireworker from Cleckheaton. Things had been going well until a bounce out from Brian's googlie delivery had landed in eye of Tony's new dog, blinding him immediately. Tony was devastated, as he had only just sprung the dog from the local takeaway the week before. His New Years' Eve destroyed, he left the pub to a tap room chorus of "two blind dogs and one world cup, dodah, dodah" and went to see what he could get for the dog from Ram Jams down Leeds Road.

Barry had also come up trumps with the fancy dress theme for the evening. Whereas other pubs in the district were messing about with the traditional tarts and vicars or celebrity lookalikes, Barry had gone for a completely different tack.

He was sick of ugly, bald housewives with varicose veins pretending to be glittery Hollywood stars, such as Marilyn Monroe, Betty Davis and Ma Sugden. When did they ever come to Bradford? No one in the Napier had even met Marilyn Monroe, except of course Sid, who had given her one behind the Bingo Hall, Mischievous Night 1956. He wanted a theme that the people of the local community could relate to. After all, Bradford has a very bright history and many things to be proud of. The author J.B. Priestley, Joe Johnson the brown snooker player, Alf Roberts and Kiki Dee, that wonderful songstress, who gave us the classic *Don't Go Breaking My Heart* with Elton John, the song that we all love so much that we can't stop vomiting blood to it. Bradford was also in the process of building its very own Argos superstore.

But Barry wanted to get beyond all the hype dished out by the various spin doctors on Bradford council. He wanted his fancy dress theme to reflect the true grit and seediness of northern life, with an emphasis on how Bradford had contributed to this.

A few people had complained about the "Come as your Favourite Serial Killer Night" but not enough to stop approximately thirteen Yorkshire Rippers, five Black Panthers, eleven Pol Pots and two Hooded Rapists filling the pub and, for the first time in about fifteen years, Barry felt contented. Obviously, Sid had let him down as usual by coming as a giant locust, believing himself to be a serial killer, but even this didn't dampen Barry's fun. He was especially pleased with Brenda who, at this very moment, was handing out souvenir claw hammers to the regulars and bleeding profusely from a neck wound.

Barry himself had combined lethal serial killer with Bradford's cosmopolitan community by coming as Bruce Lee. In a fit of intelligence, he had thought twice about covering his body with yellow food colouring but did it anyway. So what if it looked like he had jaundice for the next few weeks? It would only be like half the babies born in Bradford.

He achieved the classic Chinese eyes look by super-gluing the corners of his lids together and the kung fu battle scars were relics of an encounter with a rampant Armadillo at Knaresborough Zoo. By simply re-opening the wounds with the blade from his Bagpuss pencil sharpener, Barry had created rivers of blood, which not only added to his hardman image, but also cascaded across the wide expanse of his belly and into the eggnog, adding a certain piquancy and colour.

Brenda's sponsored "Gobbleathon" for charity, much to everyone's surprise, had also shown a profit, albeit ten pounds. She had set up a charity very dear to the hearts of the hardened drinkers of The Napier.

Over the years, the pub had seen many of its regulars reduced to shells of their former selves. Wizened old taproomers like Billy Snood, who had gallantly fought in the Great Batley Conflict 1943-1943 and Ho Dok Li, now one-hundred-and-eight, the first Vietnamese boat person in Bradford to deal in nutmeg. And others, either too dead or decapitated to mention. Many things had ravaged their bodies. Gallons of chip fat coursed through their veins blocking arteries, hissing cockroaches from Madagascar infested their substandard homes suckling off their earwax, and the local whores had not been checked for syphilis for the last twenty years.

Some of the older ones remembered a golden era when football was a man's game and a pint of mixed was as sophisticated as it got. But times had changed and it was no longer acceptable to beat the wife and sleep with the dog. Nowadays, in this modern age of man, it was the other way around. These old heroes needed guidance in their dotage and it was to help these very people that Brenda was gargling with sticky love fluid this very evening.

Brenda and Shirley, cake shop owner and slag, Spencer set up the Brenda Butlin Trust for Sad Old Bastards, or SOBs, in 1982. Off to a slow start in 1983 with their Campaign for Nuclear Incontinence, the girls had raised the astonishing sum of two hundred and thirty pounds and sixty-seven pence over the last four years. This not only funded a trotter replacement for Micky Mann, local tripe salesman and shove halfpenny champ, but also a new toaster for his granddad, who had burnt his house down by toasting crumpets with a blowtorch. Various theme nights and seaside outings had boosted coffers to such an extent, four hundred and eleven pounds in 1984, that Brenda had splashed out on a luxury boob job for Shirley.

Sick of pointing south and having to tuck her nipples into her knickers, Shirley, who qualified as a SOB on account of her grey and moulting pubic hair, was delighted to receive the very latest treatment, direct from Morecambe. This innovative seaside treatment involved implanting a couple of giant whelks into the bosom and the patient then eating tons of plankton to keep them happy and therefore still in the chest. Things went fine, with Shirley sporting a fine, firm pair of tits throughout 1985. However, since March there had been the great plankton famine of the Sargasso Sea and the whelks, now starving, had moved from the chest and were currently feeding off her pancreas. She would die shortly.

As midnight and the New Year approached, the

atmosphere was supercharged as *Make The Party Last* by the James Last Orchestra boomed out through the speakers. Everyone was up dancing, even Brenda who had passed out earlier on a cocktail of gin and ether.

The Three Amigos were also enjoying themselves. Billy had tried out his Spanish on the Tidgewell Triplets, three of the fittest girls this side of Pudsey, and unbelievably, it had worked. Four rounds of Malibu and Pineapple and the boys were in like Flynn. The Tidgewell Triplets, Suzie, Caroline and Annie, were well known as being the tightest lasses in all of Laisterdyke. Many had tried, many more had lied but none were ever satisfied. Barry Barker had once claimed a poke with Suzie behind the Co-Op but it later turned out that he was pissed and had just stuck his finger in a pot noodle. Although there was no chance of going all the way, the boys were the envy of the pub as they snuggled up to the triplets, plying them with alcohol, speed and Scampi Fries. They would probably get tit, which would be an unexpected New Year bonus as they had begun the evening with nothing. It seemed that things could not get any better until, dead on midnight, Barry pulled his masterstroke.

"Ladies and Gentlemen, Boys and Girls, Perverts and Sid, appearing live tonight at The Napier, direct from Batley Variety Club, Britain's greatest living live entertainer, Mr Versatility himself, the one, the only, Mr Roy Castle!!!"

The boys were astounded. It couldn't get any better than this. All thoughts of the Tidgewell Triplets were forgotten as Roy jumped on the bar, starting his tap dance routine and began simultaneously playing fifteen different instruments through various orifices. The folklore god of any pub singer or colliery brass band player, Roy Castle was the working man's Elvis. Like any good blacksmith, he could turn his hand to anything. Comedy, dance, magic, impressions. A true professional in a world of charlatans. Lennie Bennett, Mike and Bernie Winters and Sting.

Crooning through an Herb Alpert classic, his infectious grin spread like a prossy's thighs and very soon the whole of the pub was tapping away in time, swaying throughout the Green Room and into the Snug. As he launched into *Dedication* the pub erupted, with many of the regulars lighting up cigarettes in honour of Roy and trying to break various world records there and then.

"Dedication, Dedication, Dedication,

That's what you need.

If you want to be the best

And you want to beat the rest

Then dedication is what you need

If you want to be a Record Breaker, yeahhhhhhh"

The great man, leg akimbo across the Guinness pumps, held the final note for what seemed like hours as, in unison, the whole pub clapped and cheered. What a truly magnificent New Year's Eve and, as the clock struck the last chime, the final coup de grace. Barry's breaking his own world wanking record, with Norris and Ross McWhirter brought in with test tubes to verify. He had really pulled it off and would now be heralded as the greatest landlord of all time.

Suddenly, the beer tasted like beer and not like piss, the crisps were crispy and the Tidgewell Triplets, freed of any sexual tethers, had straddled the boys and were grinding away for England. Blue, yellow and white fireworks, Leeds colours, lit up the night and, as Hot Gossip skydived naked into the pub car park, the boys turned to each other and hugged. It had been the best time ever.

"Now Garry. Put that glass down or I will bleeding well chop you!" Barry's voice blasted out, destroying the last remnants of their New Year's Eve. The Barker Boys, Garry and Larry, had been in a bad mood all night and now they were doing what they did best; getting on people's tits and then getting the shit kicked out of themselves.

The Three Amigos looked at their beer, which had now returned to its normal consistency of golden syrup, and knew their evening was over. No doubt that the Tidgewell Triplets would probably be all tucked up in bed with a cup of hot chocolate and a guide on how to keep your virginity until you were married. Roy Castle would be away entertaining the King of Siam rather than tap dancing in a backstreet, northern pub. And of course, Barry was back to being an arsehole, barring Sid for being the only one in the pub wearing fancy dress on New Year's Eve, 1986. Poor Sid didn't even realise he was in fancy dress. He had been drinking meths since Boxing Day and just happened to turn up as Roger Moore.

This was how it normally ended. All their hard work would come to a sudden end and it was back to reality. Crap beer, a mad landlord and the Barker Boys getting a pasting. At least they didn't have to go to work tomorrow and the evening's visions would keep them going until next time. It hadn't been a bad night and there was always 1987 to look forward to.

Revision

Billy closed the enormous textbook, took a drag on his spliff and watched out of his bedroom window as an acned skateboarder collided with the pop van and crashed into Mrs Senior, the nosy neighbour from number ninety-nine. His cramming had not been going that well. It was only two months to his finals and he was still trying to get some order into his revision notes.

But how the hell was he supposed to revise?

April brought the beginning of the mating season and his dad, having incurred the wrath of the neighbourhood by pissing all over their flowers to lay his scent, was currently being held by the police for trying to mount the lollipop lady, Doreen. Billy knew things were going too far when, during *Life on Earth*, his dad quite suddenly believed himself to be a previously undiscovered species of opossum.

Billy had come home from college to find him naked in an apple tree, eating maggots and making chirping noises at a startled squirrel. It was a relief when the police took him away and charged him with impersonating a marsupial and offering hand jobs to woodland creatures. Now Billy could finally get on with some work as his dad was spending a few weeks in Menston Psychiatric Hospital, learning to bury nuts.

But just when he thought he would be able to concentrate, Billy had received a letter from his mum. He hadn't heard a thing from her since she walked out in 1977. Apparently, and how could he really ever believe her, she had married the lead singer from top Dutch rock band Golden Earring, gone on tour and had just awoken from a heroin-induced stupor that had lasted eight years. She now wanted to come home and talk to him about filo pastry and cross-stitch. He was really confused.

He had been only fifteen when she had left after the polecat spotting tour of Torremolinos, and things had changed so much since then. He had discovered vodka, genital piercing and cunnilingus and experimented with all three, although one was accidental and involved zipping up his jeans too quickly. Would she understand that he now preferred Vesta chow mein to their chicken curry range?

He wished that H was around so he could talk it through with him. He would know what was best. Danny and Mark were having their own problems at the moment and he wanted to keep their nights in the Napier special. Billy knew that her return would mean the end of his dad. She would have him committed for life as soon as she saw the collection of frogs in aspic that decorated his vest.

Spanish books, essay papers and scribbled notes lay before him like an avalanche of Latino bullshit. He was now resigned to working in Spain. The Brazilian dream had been lost about the same time as his virginity.

In 1975, all the boys in 5C at Bradford Moor Comprehensive were lusting after the blond one from Abba, or lying about how they had fingered Suzi Quatro when she just happened to do an impromptu gig at Rodley Town Hall. But Billy loved Gabriella Sabatini, the beautiful dark Argentinian tennis player and spent hours watching Wimbledon trying to catch a glimpse of her white panties as she served.

Because of his dark skin and Latino looks, inherited from his Grandad, who was exiled from Cuba by Castro for tax evasion and pimping the little whore from the Via Batistuta, Billy was quite popular with the girls in his year. The only other dark-skinned lad in the year was an Indian boy called Mick Singh, who ironically got a Saturday job with him in the mixing room at the local Almonds bakery. It was Mick who had come up with famous ditty about the aged foreman, Bill from Wigan, who was always telling the Saturday Lads to stop messing or they would end up blind, like his grandson.

"Bill is on his way to Wigan

His grandson has been blinded again

But he can't stop us

The boys from Almonds

The boys from down Gain Lane"

Even though he was popular, Billy wasn't really into the girls in his year as he struggled with their pasty skin, pimples and period pains.

But peer pressure though is a horrible thing, especially when you want to be accepted by your classmates, and Billy soon realised that he would need to let his dreams of Gabriella go, especially when all the other lads in 5C were going through Katie Marsden like there was no tomorrow. She was not a beauty by any stretch of the imagination but only charged ten pence, ten cigs and a Mars bar, which was well within the financial means of most of the boys in his year, if they laid off the heroin for a week or two. Being crap at maths, Jane had learnt to count by adding up the number of fifth formers that she had slept with and was currently reciting Pi to the power of ten.

Although for his own credibility, Billy knew it was important not to get left behind in the sexual stakes but, being a sensitive lad, he had always planned for his first time to be a personal experience with a girl that he at least fancied a bit, and not like Alan Mitchell, the physics geek in 5C, and whose nickname was "Seven Up" after a particularly busy day for Katie.

The only girl that he half fancied was called Jane Staincliffe. She was the Head Girl for the year and the best at French, maths, English, geography and school champion in everything from the one hundred metres to British Bulldogs. She also had very big nipples and wore tight, black, corduroy trousers that put the V into Very Shapely Muff. On a few occasions, he had tried to impress her during lessons by answering questions correctly, but this had proved too difficult as Billy was pretty rubbish at most subjects. But obviously he was the best in class at Spanish and had played that card to such an effect that Jane agreed to go to the 1978 Easter School Disco with him.

There are many great Yorkshire traditions and getting totally wankered before a school disco is one of them. Billy would go around to Danny's house and fill a Schweppes bottle with a little drop of everything from Danny's Mum's drinks cabinet. Gin, whisky, Advocaat, Blue Bols, crème de menthe, vodka, cherry brandy, Clan Dew, Cinzano Bianco, Blue Stratos, Cinzano Rosso and Cinzano Rose, Stone's ginger wine, Black Beer, vodka, Drambuie, Pernod and a good slug of Watney's Party Seven.

Being pissed enough to dance was a sign of maturity at

school discos and usually meant that you got a snog at the end of the night. Unfortunately, shoulder bopping to Mud and Showaddywaddy, and the newly invented pogoing to the Boomtown Rats and Sex Pistols, meant you were always sick. Usually down the throat of the girl you ended up snogging with to Foreigner, Chicago or some other shit band like that.

But Billy wasn't going to do that with Jane. He wanted to remain sober so he could tell her how much he really admired her, how much he wanted to be with her and, if on the off chance that she was game, so he could finger her.

The evening had gone well. Billy was wearing his best Van Heusen shirt, quite a hit when the rest of 5C were sweating their bollocks off in Star Jumpers, his Brut aftershave wasn't too pungent, Jane had laughed at his joke about Fidel and the Blind Donkey and she had not been averse to bumping groins to *Solid As A Rock* by Ashford and Simpson, even when he'd got lobbed up. They found a quiet corner in the school gym and the conversation flowed through various topics until inevitably he moved it onto sex.

"I'd really like to see you again Jane. Do you fancy coming round next Wednesday night? My dad is visiting Great Aunt Carmen on the Manchester Ship Canal. We can listen to some records in my room." he whispered, his hand moving gently around her shoulder until it rested upon her left breast.

"And I'd like to see you again Billy," she replied, quickly removing his hand, "but my belief in Jesus means that I will only go out with a fellow Christian who can share my joy of being at one with Our Lord." She looked deep into his eyes, her desire obvious and then compounded as her tongue grazed his cheek.

Living with a mad dad and a slut whore Mum meant that Billy had never been to a proper Christian church before. He had made a brief appearance at a Sunday school in Thornbury cricket pavilion but that had simply been a picture of Christ hung above a few discarded cricket pads and a Sir Geoffrey Boycott annual.

And so, it was with a little trepidation that he first entered St James the Great on Easter Sunday, hand in hand with Jane. Billy sat down and watched in wonderment as the Vicar and the congregation drank some wine, sang hymns and praised Jesus. Jane kept a tight grip on his hand throughout, often turning to smile and reassure him that everything was OK. He felt elated, as if life had taken on new meaning and purpose. The sun glowed through the stained glass and beams of light danced around Jane's golden hair like a halo. She was an angel. When it came to prayers, he felt himself kneeling forward and joining in, as if some other greater force was guiding him.

Which, of course, it was. Lust. Christ Almighty he was fucking bored! Even more bored than when his Uncle Pedro came round to tell his lies about joining the Buena Vista Social Club on their tour of Guantanamo Bay. The Vicar kept banging on for hours about these dead people, who he had never heard of, and who sounded really dull. Just walking around the desert, following Jesus and listening to his crap about being nice to everyone, when we all know that you should always hate Man U.

But, if being pious for a couple of hours a week, meant him getting his end away with Jane, then he would be confirmed, anointed, baptised, whatever. Jane was really opening up to him and he had even copped a feel of her nipples during a Christian Youth Club disco. They were developing a real relationship. He was helping her with her Spanish, while she was helping him with his maths, physics, chemistry, English, geography, French, art and biology. Most of his mates in 5C now called him Lazarus and took the piss by making crosses in woodwork and then sticking them to the back of his school blazer with Bostick. Only Danny really knew the score and he was taking side bets with the lads on when Billy would bang her.

"I'm really starting to trust you Billy and I really value our friendship," Jane rested her head on his shoulder, as they lay together on the warm grass, the July sun slowly sinking over Bradford Moor Park, "and I want our relationship to go further. Although we are only fifteen, I feel that I am ready for some deeper commitment."

Billy immediately felt himself stirring, like the time Gabriella had accidently tripped during a rally with Chrissie Evert and he had got the full gusset shot, but he remained cool and simply leant over to brush the hair from her eyes.

"I have never felt like this about anybody, except Jesus of course, and I would really love you to be the one." She gazed into his eyes, looking for a reaction but he remained calm and aloof. "Please say you will Billy, I don't want it to be anybody but you."

His jeans were now stretched so tight that he felt that he would pass out but he had done it. All those long, long prayers and trying to not laugh during sermons, and all that shit about being nice to everybody. It had worked and now he would be able to stride proudly into Sharp's chemist, ask for three featherlite johnnies and become the envy of the whole of the fifth year. Danny had talked about screen printing some T-shirts with "I shagged Jane Staincliffe" on but even he had thought this a little insensitive and would be completely happy with the adulation of his peers.

"Only if you are sure. I wouldn't want to rush you." Billy knew there and then that the Christian religion couldn't be real as he would have surely been struck down by God's thunderbolt for telling that lie. "My Dad is out tomorrow night and I have got a bottle of Cinzano Bianco in my room."

"No Billy, I was thinking about having a party at my house so we could announce our engagement to all our friends and family. I want everyone to know how much I love you and how happy we will be when we are married."

His jeans suddenly became very, very slack and he knew he could be on the verge of blowing three months hard work. He made myself count to ten and then thought very carefully about his next few words.

"But Jane, don't you think that before we make a commitment, such as marriage, we should find out if we are sexually compatible? I know lots of people who have divorced because they have not been able to satisfy each other sexually." He really tried to keep the panic and pleading from his voice.

"But with the commitment that you have made to Christ then I know we will be brilliant together and I can't wait for our wedding night when we do it."

For a second, he felt himself go stiff again but he was now too desperate to notice, or even care. "But Jane, it will really hurt on our, your wedding night if you leave it till then. Why don't we have a go now just to see what it is like and then your,

our wedding night will be even more special." He realised what he was saying but was too far gone to care.

"My hymen has already spilt due to my hurdling, so it will be brilliant on the night." Jane smiled at him and, at that very moment, he knew that he was beaten. A girl who knew that her hymen had broken, whatever the fuck that is, was more than a match for him. Billy had only recently read about what the clit was for! He tried to smile but inside he felt dead.

Like Jesus.

A week later at Danny's house, he got absolutely leathered on Pils Snakebite, got lucky, or unlucky, and attained the nickname of Bottle, as in ten green bottles, as in ten, as in the last of a Katie Marsden promotional night. Jane had found out and called off the engagement immediately, even though he didn't actually remember getting engaged. According to her best mate, she had cried for two days solid, which made Billy feel slightly better, but had then emerged bitter and twisted, hating Jesus for letting her down and she had gone and shagged Alan Mitchell, physics geek, behind the school lab just to get back at him. Not a very Christian act and not one that pleased Danny as the tight bastard physics geek wouldn't even buy the "I shagged Jane" t-shirts off him.

And so ended his brief flirtation with Christianity. And Katie Marsden, who actually paid her own way through Oxford, so fair play to her. But just to piss Jane off, he had continued with Spanish through O and A level, as it was the only thing he was better than her at.

But now, as his finals approached, he questioned why he was bothering at all. He had been to Spain about five times, including the infamous Donkey Bonk Tour of 84, and realised that every bloody one in Spain spoke near perfect English. So why was he spending all this time learning Spanish when all he had to do was improve his English by saying "Harrogate" instead of "Arrowgut"? And what was so special about Spain? It was just a slightly warmer version of Morecambe but with all day drinking, oily tasting chips and the shits. Even the Barker Boys had been, although they had been deported after three days and had their passports confiscated for leering, vomiting and sporting too much white flesh in a public place.

He knew he would have to get himself motivated, but like a very strict heterosexual, he just couldn't be arsed.

Bother

Danny guessed that he was about to receive his final, final, final written warning. Stood in the office, listening to Mr Tally, company director and racist, bang on about discipline, loyalty and the state of British youth, he was reminded of the scene from *Kes*, where all the boys, including a completely innocent one, get caned for smoking. Mr Tally, who had been part of the factory since Joan Collins had first lost her virginity, looked stern and talked of halcyon days when men were proud to be engineers and hard work was an ethic.

"Those days were tough. I remember losing a finger in the grinding mill late one Wednesday evening. I had been working solid since Monday, as all the family had diphtheria, rickets and ringworm, and since Father had been sliced in two by an errant plough, I was the only wage earner. Doctors were not cheap. Well anyway, to cut a long story short, I mixed a bit of flour and water and stuck the finger back on so I could finish the shift. It smarted a little when I dipped it in the furnace to cauterise the blood but did I moan? Did I slacken? Did I buggery!"

Danny fought back the urge to laugh as he looked at Mr Tally's third finger on his left hand. It was completely black and as bent as John Inman.

"And then, of course, gangrene set in. I remember doing an eighty-seven-hour shift smelling like a darkie's plimsoll.

People wouldn't go near me as I stank so much. I had to eat my lard and bread out in the yard, in fifteen foot of snow, naked, as the council had re-possessed all my clothes due to non-payment of Poverty Tax. I thought about going to the hospital to have the gangrene treated but the hospital was twenty-seven miles away and I only had enough shoe leather left to walk twenty-five." Tally pointed to photograph of the works outing to Morecambe in 1936.

"You see those men Danny. Solid as steel those men. I would have let any of them have sex with my daughter, or borrow my Black and Decker Workmate, or glance through my backlog of Bradford City programmes. Look at them lad!"

Danny tore his gaze from the mass scrap in the yard between the Pakistanis and Indians, and looked at the photo.

"Tell me. What do you see in the eyes of those men?" Danny looked hard at the picture.

"I see a load of blokes who are dirty and look completely pissed off about having to spend a day in Morecambe without any cash to buy beer or dope and no chance of shagging anything tasty as women in those days hadn't heard of feminine hygiene and didn't even give blowjobs."

Tally sighed as he sat down at his desk, opened the top drawer and removed Danny's file.

"You really are a proper little bastard. People told me that you are a wrong 'un but I was prepared to give you the benefit of the doubt, as I knew your father. He was a good worker. Always on time. Never asking for a pay rise."

"Yeah, and look where that fucking got him! Bronchitis and asbestos poisoning! Three fucking grand in compensation, which we had to use to pay for his funeral, a wreath worth about two bob from the firm and, of course Mr Tally, some nice but totally fucking meaningless words from you about what a good bloke he was!" He had been with his dad when he had died and nobody understood the pain that he had gone through at the end.

"I'll choose to ignore that lad. Your father wouldn't like you talking like this. He understood a day's work for a day's pay. Not like you. Look at the state of this file. I've got more on you than the rest of the factory put together. Look at this..."

Danny once again turned to watch the fight outside. It was getting good. Not only had the knuckle-dusters come out but also one of the Indians was swinging a full-size Samurai sword above his head. Someone would have to stop these lunchtime cricket matches.

Tally began to read from the file.

7/6/79 — Verbal warning for putting Mr Tally's tartan thermos in the incinerator, claiming it was an incendiary device from the East Fife branch of the IRA

10/12/80 — Verbal warning for calling site foreman Peter Thompson, "a complete and utter useless twat" in full view of the canteen, accompanied by a two-fingered salute of well-known origin and meaning

24/12/80 — Written warning for tying up Peter Thompson and illuminating his rear end by inserting a string of fourteen Christmas lights into his anus

18/8/81 — Verbal warning for inciting a riot by telling the Asian workforce that the term "blackleg" was a derogatory managerial reference aimed at them to highlight their unwashed feet

3/11/82 — Written warning for setting off fireworks in the main production site, leading to an evacuation of the factory and an early start to Diwali, the Hindu Festival of Light, with one quarter of the workforce then taking an unscheduled day off

5/7/84 — Verbal warning for three days unauthorised absence. Claimed to have been abducted and held hostage by the Bradford branch of the Palestinian Liberation Organisation, PLO, for non-payment of subs

22/12/85 — Written warning for obscene behaviour at the company's Kids Christmas Disco. Appeared drunk and naked with a sprig of mistletoe attached to his genitalia, asking the canteen staff for Christmas kisses

12/10/86 — Final written warning for making Kung Fu death stars in factory hours to sell to a particular football firm for inappropriate usage

"So tell me what happened this time?"

Of course, it had been another dull day at Radebe Engineering and to alleviate the boredom, Andy, Danny's best mate at work and part time balloon dancer, had suggested playing at Dodge the Chuck Key. A favourite but highly dangerous game, it involved starting up his lathe with the chuck key still in and then dodging it as it flew past your head and into the wall behind. Safety goggles could be worn but that was for lasses.

It was two-two and both Andy and Danny were in top form. Andy did have a slight graze to his ear, when he was distracted by the morning call to Mecca. Also, the picture of a naked Princess Margaret on the wall behind the lathe did have a few more holes than would be usually assumed of royalty. But it had been a tight game and slight injuries were to be expected. It was Danny's turn and the boys agreed to turn up the lathe speed to the max. This was for real pros and had only previously been attempted by Johnny "One-Eye" Wood, now a Stevie Wonder tribute singer and ex-lathe worker.

The lathe was primed for two thousand rpm and as Andy placed the key in drill lock, he softly spoke the Vietnamese incantation from the Russian roulette scene in *The Deerhunter*. Danny tied the customary greasy hankie around his head and primed himself for the push of the red button that would release the deadly missile. Andy began the countdown.

"Five"

Danny wiped a bead of sweat from his brow and set his position. "Four"

He fixed his gaze, William Tell like, on the silver arrow aimed at his head. "Three"

The whole factory seemed to go deathly quiet. "Two"

Andy's finger moved towards the red trigger. "One"

"What the fuck are you two up to now?" Peter Thompson, foreman and part-time Christmas decoration, strode into the workroom just as Andy's finger hit the button. Danny, his concentration broken, hit the floor like a pissed-up Irishman as the chuck key rocketed from the lathe, ricocheted off the Karen Carpenter Dietary Calendar, smashed against Andy's A-Team lunchbox and ploughed into the groin area of aforementioned Peter Thompson.

As in the lyrics of the great ABC song, "Tears are not enough". Blood, urine, a little bit of spunk and a lot more blood were most definitely a better description of the state of Peter

Thompson's knackers, as he grovelled on the floor, the chuck key still lodged in his copious scrotum. Andy, sprang into life, awakened by the screams and quite coarse language of Thompson, and offered him his pack of Handy Andies. Danny ran towards the First Aid box, slipped on one of Thompson's liberated testicles and crashed into Nurse Mary, who roused from her gin-induced stupor, popped the testicle in her pocket and began to apply dressings to the wounded foreman.

"Fancy a cig Danny?" Andy pulled out a packet of Regal King Size and walked towards the factory door.

"Yeah, alright." Danny had been trying to give them up but the sight of Thompson had got to him. "I've really dropped a bollock this time," he thought, as he lit up.

"You do realise that, because of your juvenile antics, it is highly unlikely that Peter Thompson will ever father children again. Which to be frank, it is a good thing. He has seven already and they are all ugly little bastards. However, that is beside the point. I have spoken to Andy already and he has agreed on a written warning. But what can I do with you Danny?" Tally had now stood up and was obviously going into serious talk mode.

Danny looked out of the window again. The fight had now stopped and, although, there were a few pools of blood in the yard, Pakistan had restarted their innings and were sixty-five for three, Zulfikhar Hussein, top batsman and paint sprayer, twenty-eight not out.

A National Express coach passed down Stickler Lane, destination unknown but anywhere but Bradford. Danny thought of H, probably at this very moment lighting up a King Edward in a Bedouin tent. He should have gone but he knew it wouldn't have worked. Something was going to come along.

Billy and Mark felt it as well and their pictures were getting more and more vivid. Things were going to change, and if he could just hang on to his job for a few months longer and keep going to the Napier, he knew it would be fine.

"I don't know what to do with you. In the one hundred and twenty-seven years that Radebe Engineering has been up and running we have only ever sacked one person. And you know who that was." It was rumoured that in 1915 a young Austrian, on work experience from the sister factory in Munich, had been dismissed for letting off gas canisters in the canteen. "When you are with us, you are a good worker. But can you change Danny?" Tally looked straight at him.

"OK Mr Tally. But keep Thompson away from me."

"I don't think Peter will have the balls to mess with you again. But Danny, this is the final, final warning. Any more pissing about and you will be out of here faster than Jesse Owens on speed. Do I make myself clear?"

"Yes, Sir." Danny left the office and went off to find Andy in the toilets. He needed some cash from the Three-Card Brag game if he was to go to the Napier tonight. He stopped and bent down to pick up the cricket ball to throw back to Imran Nazir, top leg spinner and foundry man. But, strangely, it wasn't a cricket ball as it was too small and purple in colour and as, Nurse Mary crossed the yard, blood dripping out of a large hole in her pocket, Danny felt a whole lot better.

Hospital

It had been a difficult month for Mark. He was back in the casualty department of Bradford Royal Infirmary. Amanda, fired up on Special Brew and tripe, had fractured his jaw during a heated argument on whether to upgrade to giant sausages in batter or keep to standard size. Being from Cornwall, he was only pixie small and no match for her Joe Bugner left hook, which was legendary among the Fish Fryers Association and Reeperbahn pimps. The police wanted him to press charges, because they hated her as well, but he decided to let it pass. Prison wouldn't have any positive effect on Amanda. She would simply come out a top dog lesbian, look him up and sit on his face until he suffocated on the Brillo pad of acrid wire that was her pubic hair.

Laid in a hospital bed, surrounded by copies of the *Angling Times*, with front-page pictures of Mad Alf Reeday's twelve-pound tench, he actually felt quite happy. He had a bit of time to himself to think about where he was, what he was doing, and what he was going to do next.

Amanda and her fat sister Stephanie were running the shop, which meant that profits would be down, but Billy had promised to look in after college to make sure that they were actually serving some customers and not eating everything themselves. Mark had once been on a day trip to Goole to review the price of cod and she had gone through the entire year's stock of pickled onions.

Mark knew that it couldn't go on like this. He was only twenty-six but already he had been in hospital with a fractured arm, cracked ribs, a broken nose and crushed nuts. He was certain that she would kill him one day, just like she had murdered his tropical fish. Why she was jealous of a couple of dozen angelfish and neon tetras, he would never know. She had said it was because he loved them more than her and that he never bought her daphnia. Anyway, one day he had come back from the wholesalers to find "Tropical Fish Bits" on the menu, the batter flavoured with Tabasco to give them more of a Caribbean taste. She had always been insanely jealous of him, even decking her bridesmaid on their wedding day for calling him "love".

But her obsessive behaviour had really kicked off after the annual Napier trip to Morecambe in 1983. It was Mark's first time and, although Billy and Danny had warned him about what could happen, he wasn't at all prepared for the horror, shame and ensuing violence.

Napier pub trips to Morecambe were famous throughout Bradford for the ferocity of the drinking, fighting and the sordid sex games that usually followed. Many of the boys would pre-book appointments at the VD clinic in anticipation of what might happen and, every year, Johnny Moore would put himself down for a liver transplant just in case it packed in during the seven-hour dark mild session. One year, Morecambe was closed due to a typhoid and cholera epidemic but the boys still went, adding to the local misery by introducing dysentery and pox.

As always, Barry was the Master of Ceremonies on the

trip and would be suitably attired in Hawaiian shirt, shorts and "Kiss Me Dick" hat. Drinking would start at eight thirty a.m. with a complimentary pint of Bucks Fizz, or Pomagne and Kia-Ora due to Barry being such a tight twat and a general lack of appreciation for anything fizzy and French.

Bottles would be served throughout the coach journey with in situ entertainment being provided by Shirley, cake shop owner and slag, Spencer's daughter, Miranda, who had once had a trial with Bradford Northern rugby league team and could take a full one and a half pounds of black pudding. A few of the lads never even made it to Morecambe, as failure to drink or any vomiting, including watery burps, meant the guilty party would be debagged, shaved and left to die in Settle, a place that never should have existed.

Mark had prepared himself carefully for the trip and, as advised by Billy, had been eating nothing but lard for the last week. Lining the stomach was vital for the consumption of Barry's Bucks Fizz, dark mild and fanny batter. He had managed to keep down Brenda's pre-trip fry up of bacon and kidney in a white wine sauce, drunk the obligatory gallon of brown ale, sung along with the George Formby medley and, all in all, felt pretty good as the coach pulled into Morecambe's impressive municipal car park.

The Bradford Arms was a quaint oldy-worldy pub, owing much to the fact that it hadn't been decorated since Henry II played bar billiards against Friar Tuck in 1157. It had been opened in 45BC by a caveman from Pontefract, who had meant to go to Bradford to buy Woolly Mammoth steaks, got lost and hitchhiked on the back of a brontosaurus to Morecambe. There, he had formed a union with a Celt and the

Bradford Arms Public House was born, serving frothy ale and meat pies to passing dignitaries, lepers and shag merchants.

Passed down the family line over the centuries, the current owner, the twenty-seventh Earl of Monkey Spunk, was a strange character who collected tab ends and loved Mexican food. However, he always welcomed the boys from Bradford, as if it was their second home, which of course it was. It's dark, dank atmosphere and overwhelming smell of crow pie and horseshit added to the sombre mood for the first of many challenges, set by MC Barry, for the travelling men of the Napier.

The day was designed around complete debauch, with every excess catered for. There was the bareknuckle shove ha'penny contest, the pull an ugly bird competition and a vast variety of drinking games, including sink the pink and pissbottle, that all-time favourite.

However, just as the contestants were lining up for the qualifying heats of Nob Burn, a test of mind over matter and sandpaper endurance, Tommy burst in and announced that Morecambe town centre was affected by a power cut. Immediately the whole pub emptied. The Napier lads knew they were on to a winner. Donning balaclavas, ski hats and Geoffrey Boycott masks, they set off for the local jewellers, pawn shops and boulangerie. If free French sticks were on offer, then these boys wanted to be part of it.

They returned with their spoils an hour later, as a little man in a Morecambe office put the plug back in and the lights came back on. A little too early for Dirk Brown, dominoes team captain and crane fly enthusiast, who was caught with his tongue in a croissant and executed on the spot by

76

Morecambe's Red Brigade.

Adidas bags overflowed with the riches of a small Lancastrian seaside resort. Souvenir silver teaspoons and ashtrays, a wide assortment of flavoured rock, a dozen jars of pickled cockles, one or two ugly birds and of course, a donkey. Barry was extremely proud of this acquisition, as it wasn't even dark when he'd nicked it off the beach. He now walked it around the pub as if in the Ascot parade ring, the boys betting on how long it would take before it shat on the floor.

The day progressed in a haze and, although Mark still felt fairly good, the booze and speed were fighting each other and he didn't know whether to have a kip on the beach or to run the New York marathon. He knew that he would be OK when the candyfloss that he had won at the Pleasure Beach had a chance to kick in.

As veterans of the outing, Billy and Danny had this year become honorary members of the Napier Synchronised Swimming Team in a classic interpretation of Kingsley's *Water Babies*. Although the sea had been a little choppy, and they had lost Brian Dibble, the kinky wireworker from Cleckheaton, in quicksand, the performance had been outstanding. In fact, the Lord Mayor of Morecambe had voted it the best ever show, even topping their 1974 version of the *Ziegfeld Follies*, with a special guest appearance from Esther Williams and Mark Spitz. To be part of this team was a top accolade, albeit they would definitely now contract cholera from venturing into the sea.

At ten p.m., after changing into their white jackets, black shirts and white leather ties, the boys and the rest of the coach party bribed their way into Morecambe's top nightclub,

Dollars and Dimes. This was the annual location for the last and most prestigious challenge of the outing, the Pull An Ugly Bird competition.

Mark was very keen to win this and wanted to go one better than his second place in the Whelk Flicking contest. He had a proven record in pulling ugly birds and his C.V. (crass vulgarity) was bursting with horror bags, including Katie from his time at sea, a school dinner lady and, of course, the big fat ugly bitch that he was now married to. Danny and Billy had put their last tenner on him to win at odds of three to one, although they both knew that this year, 1983, heralded the return of the master.

Paul "Rambi" Robinson was the undisputed champion, having won the title an unprecedented eight years on the trot. He also held the all-time most perverse act after felching an incontinent fishwife from Blackpool. His winners included a cockney with a glass eye on her hen night, half a Siamese twin and Penelope Keith.

The dyed chest hair and nob-shaped medallion were just part of his repertoire, which included the now legendary "Alright Love, do you shag?" His body, ravaged by years of antibiotics, jealous husbands and being under fat birds, now stood proud on the dance floor, as he studied the form. Mark was worried.

The place was filling up and Barry was pleased at the turn out. A woman's bear baiting team from Queensbury had lowered the tone considerably and a few of the gang were already making moves towards them. Barry never took part in the competition, as he had to remain objective about judging the winner, very much like a young Eric D. Morley in the Miss

World competition.

The Three Amigos had been drinking for about fourteen hours and, although they were all pissed, they were still standing and ready for the hunt. Danny had approached one of the Queensbury girls earlier but even the thought of winning the coveted prize couldn't force him to snog someone who smoked John Player Specials and was called Gladys. Billy, having won the title last year, when Rambi was having genital warts removed, was playing it very cool. He knew how much Mark wanted to win the title and was therefore acting as his coach tonight.

He had learned over the years that the secret of this competition was not to move in too quickly. As in any school disco, all the fit birds go first and it is only the really ugly ones who are left sitting in corners as the slow records start. He could sense Mark's nervousness and his impatience at not having made a move on anyone, when others around him were copping off with some real gruellers.

"What about her?" Mark pointed at an albino postmistress from Wigan.

"No way. Look at her body. She must be a thirty-six twenty-four thirty-six and, even if she has pink eyes, Barry would find her attractive." Billy lit a joint and passed it to Mark. He knew that Mark needed to relax a bit. It was a big occasion. His first major Pull An Ugly Bird competition and nerves were bound to play a part.

"Don't panic. When I won the title, it was on the last song. Everybody had written me off and then I saw her, crouching in a dark corner".

"Yeah Mark, you wouldn't believe it, "Danny said, "eighteen stone, only one finger on her left hand and dressed in a milkmaid's outfit. Class."

"I know, but both of you have backed me and, look at Rambi." He pointed to the dance floor, where Rambi was licking green mucus from the nose of a Mancunian bus conductress with inflamed adenoids. "How can I beat that?"

"Rambi is past it. I have been engaged to uglier birds than that." Billy knew that he had to raise his confidence. "He is all show with his Old Spice and pubic wig. His day has gone mate."

"Rambi is getting too choosy." added Danny. "Rumour has it that he turned down Wendy does Wyke last week, and even Barry has been there."

The dance floor cleared as *Lucky Stars* by Dean Friedman came on, leaving only pissed up couples hanging on to each other. This gave the boys a clearer view of the booths surrounding the club and it was in the far corner that Billy spotted the winner.

"Quick, over there." He pointed towards a glint of silver metal in the purple strobe light. Danny gasped in disbelief as she was wheeled into view. Half Chinese and half Antarctician, she was sipping mild through a straw as her jaw was wired up and her arms were heavily bound in a homemade straight jacket. "Marky, there's your prize!"

The nurse came into his room and asked what he wanted for lunch. He handed her his completed menu card and she left. He had been married to Amanda for about five years after meeting her on a mackerel fishing tour of Cleethorpes in '81. It hadn't been 'love at first sight' but she had let him shag her in the fish-gutting factory and then she had stuck to him like a persistent bogey. Marriage had increased her violent streak and the phone call from Wicki Wicki Wheels had obviously sent her over the edge.

Of course, it was Danny's fault. He was the one who had slipped Mark's phone number into the folds of her straight jacket as Barry presented him with the trophy. Maybe out of jealousy? Mark didn't know. He was in no fit state to care at the time, high on both the number of joints it had taken him to snog her and from the delirious adulation shown by the rest of the lads. He was swept along with the euphoria of the moment, carried out of the club on the shoulders of Barry and Rambi and then congratulated all the way back to Bradford on the coach. It was Billy, who had christened her Wicki Wicki Wheels after a racehorse that he had once backed, and it stuck with chorus after chorus of,

"Oh Wicki Wicki
Wicki Wicki Wicki Wicki Wicki Wheels"

on the coach all the way back to Bradford.

Amanda had never trusted him since then, even though he had claimed that she was a long-long relative from Antarctica, who had gone mad when a Chinese man had run her over in his rickshaw. She hadn't believed him and broke his arm. He knew things had to change. And it was. Each night in the pub, the pictures were getting more and more vivid and both he and the two others felt that something big was going to happen very soon.

Fitcrack

The Napier had never been more in love.

Her name was Sarah and she was posh. Not really posh as in changing her blouse every shift or using a fork to eat tinned fruit salad with real pineapple chunks, but posh enough to make Barry scrape the grime from his cleavage and Sid to change the sesame seed oil in his hair. For a start she said "water" instead of "watter", used soft toilet paper instead of Izal and her parents owned their own terraced house in Shipley.

It had been a real coup for Barry. He knew that he would be in stiff competition with Archie Shag, the landlord from The Miners Inn, and Bobby Jewell, sun-tanned impresario from The Lizards Crutch, Bradford's premier lounge saloon with two choices of lager and the singing talents of Lorenzo Pavorotti, pizza waiter and crooner to the stars.

However, he had outbid them both at the last moment, chucking in a year's supply of cheesy footballs, an utter bombshell among bar snack initiatives, in order to secure her services.

It was only the second time he had ever bid for anything from the Bradford Annual Barmaid Auctions and this time he was confident that he was on to a winner. The first time he had been duped into buying a blind cleaner from an asbestos factory, who kept banging into the optics and coughing up blood over the customers. Brenda had not been pleased, especially as he had only gone out to buy *The Sun* and a slab of Wensleydale cheese.

She had been the last lot and was far and away the best. Barry had been thinking about getting some help behind the bar for a while as Brenda's humming minge was beginning to flavour the bitter.

She came with excellent references, a Master's Degree in Lime Cordial, a bleached blonde rinse and best of all, she was currently studying to be a nurse. Barry's favourite TV programme was *Angels* and he was still madly in love with Nurse Marge, a wizened, old sister who had treated his ingrown left nipple when he was eight.

During the auction itself, each barmaid on offer was required to perform a series of assessed bar duties, including mopping up vomit, fondling the pumps suggestively and throwing out a drunken darts team at last orders. She had done all three with gusto, with the darts team actually crawling out of the mock pub on their hands and knees, salivating like wild dogs and rolling over to have their beer bellies tickled.

Barry had spent his entire annual clothing and tripe allowance on the bid but, as he surveyed the bar, he knew that she was worth it. Beer sales had doubled in the two weeks that Sarah had worked. Condom sales had tripled, as she was so skilled in making all the sad bastards think they stood a chance, and the dominoes team had started to wear surgical masks, like the Millwall firm F-Troop, in tribute to her beauty and vocation.

Barry had thought that Brenda would have been jealous but even she was pleased. With the extra takings, she had been able to splash out on a set of fishing lures and a new luncheon meat bait, guaranteed to catch carp and roach, and had already booked a mackerel trip to Whitby with Shirley, who was now completely emaciated as the whelks ate away at her liver.

Brenda wasn't the slightest bit jealous of Sarah. She knew that she could still turn on the taproom lads with her corn on the lob impression and as for Barry straying? Well, he'd been waking up to sticky pyjamas for the last week or two and Brenda knew that he'd be satisfied with that.

"So what will it be tonight Sid?" Sarah licked her lips suggestively and laid her hand on the liver-spotted, nicotine stained fingers of the Great One. Sid's Adam's apple bobbed up and down like a whore's arse as he struggled to speak.

"Half a mild, Sarah my darling, and take one for yourself." Barry resisted the urge to piss himself laughing. He just pissed himself instead.

Sid had never bought anyone a drink in forty years, even including the time when a dehydrated naked super model, who had just walked across the Sahara Desert, wandered deliriously into the pub offering full sex to anyone who would give her just a sip of their lemonade. If she had that effect on Sid, the man who hired out his biro to people filling in Kidney Donor Cards, then things would never be the same again. He had already noticed a difference in the taproom, where Blue Stratos and Brylcreem had replaced the usual smell of horse liniment and stale sweat.

Brian Dibble, the kinky wireworker from Cleckheaton, had surgically removed the "I Love Lucy" tattoo from his forearm with some wet and dry sandpaper, and crudely gouged out "Sarah is Fit" on his chest with a nail file. Even Tony's new dog, Cyclops, deafened by an impromptu version of *Whole Lotta Rosie* by the local scout troop, had crawled out from beneath his usual hiding place under the pool table and was currently humping away at her white stockinged leg. The good times were back and Barry was certain the Napier would feature in next month's *Moderately Good Pub Guide.*

The Three Amigos had also noticed the new barmaid and were today all sporting their Sunday best football shirts. Billy had his England '86 red shirt on, Danny his Scotland '86 blue and Mark his Argentina '86 blue and white stripes.

Mark had supported Argentina during the Falklands because Thatcher had snatched away clotted cream from Cornish schoolchildren, and he was the only lad in Bradford to have the full set of General Galtieri Panini Stickers. They had bought the shirts on a day trip to Scarborough to see their mad mate Fang, who had emigrated there to escape the shackles of inner-city architecture. They looked sharp amongst the rest of the 1872 Bradford Park Avenue away kits in the Green Room.

"She must like football. She's a nurse." Billy was smashed. In fact, all three of them had been pissed every night since Sarah had started, as their trips to the bar had suddenly become twice as frequent.

"Why must she like football?" Mark, as usual, was the only one who could retain the power of logic after nine pints.

"Yeah, why?" Danny joined in, just to see if he could still talk.

"Well nurses deal with sick people, so they must like them. Man U fans are sick. Therefore, nurses must like Man U fans. Therefore, nurses like football." Billy sat back on the bench, a satisfied glow across his face. Danny nodded. He was convinced and wiped the ash from the collar of his Scotland shirt, before aiming an extremely sexy look toward Sarah behind the bar. Well it would have been sexy if both eyes had been pointing the same way. Mark wasn't so sure.

"OK, if we take your idea forward Einstein, then all nurses like serial killers." Mark had eaten rice and peas for tea and was feeling very clever tonight.

"No," replied Billy, "because serial killers are not sick, they are just confused. Nurses don't like confused people as it makes it harder to get them better because no one understands what is wrong with them. Look at Rasputin. Monk or mass murderer? He couldn't choose. The Black Panther. Bradford's top door to door brush salesman or sub post office thief and heiress killer?"

"Yeah, that's why nurses don't like Adam Ant," Danny spluttered, "because he could never decide if he was a dandy highwayman, a pirate or Prince Charming. Nurses like things nice and simple. Like a cut to mend or a leg to rub." Mark thought about replying but then decided all three were too wrecked to carry on with this particular intellectual train of thought.

"I wonder if she is a natural blond and the collar matches the cuffs?" Mark decided to get back onto more familiar ground.

"I don't think so," said Billy. "I've been studying her root activity for a couple of days now and there has definitely been a darkening towards the crown. Anyway, I don't really like blond muff."

"No, me neither. It's a bit like going down on a Shredded

Wheat." Danny had an aversion to cereal-based pubic hair, much preferring the slightly burnt toast look of a brunette bush. "I bet that it's a tan shade of brown."

"Like the nutty, chestnut brown of half an ounce of St Bruno ready rubbed."

"Or the soft, silky auburn brown of a squirrel's brush."

"Or the dark, almost earthy brown of the 1975 Coventry City away kit, you know the one made by Admiral, which copied the Wales home kit."

She knew the three boys were talking about her, as they kept glancing towards the bar and then making holes with the thumb and index fingers of their right hands and sticking the index finger of their left hand in and out of the hole very quickly. She didn't mind. Working in a pub and being a nurse meant that she was used to all types of sexual innuendo, and the Napier crew were completely sad desperados. Lost souls on a sea of perpetual ineptitude.

However, the three in the corner were slightly different. They said please and thank you, had their own teeth and didn't permanently salivate and masturbate every time she bent down to empty the drip tray. She had been watching them for a few days now and thought the married one looked a bit sad, the one with the wanky student clothes, a bit mad, and the hungry looking keen one, a bit bad.

"I bet she likes it spread all over, really thick."

The conversation had now moved on to whether Mother Teresa used Stork margarine instead of butter.

"Fuck this," said Billy, who had lost interest in Mother Theresa when he'd found out that she was a religious leader in India rather than a buxom porn star from Harlem, "I am going

87

to ask her out."

Mark and Danny put their hands behind their heads, leant back on their chairs and watched in awe as Billy began his world-famous chat up technique. World famous because it was absolutely shit. He tucked his green Israeli combat trousers into his calf-high black suede boots, a bad start, and wiped pork scratching residue off his paisley t-shirt which he wore under his football shirt, an even worse start, a bygone from the time when he wanted to be Morrissey. He then sauntered like a young Marlon Brando towards the bar.

"Can I have three pints of bitter and all of your loving baby?"

Billy must have been really pissed to use that one thought Mark, as Danny projectile vomited over half of the Green Room. He'd last used it on the ugliest barmaid in the world from the High Flyer, and even she had twatted him. If there had been any chance with Sarah, he had now completely blown it. Even Sid, who had invented the line, shook his head in disappointment. You couldn't just use it with anyone. It had to be with a guaranteed cert, like Mary, who was dead.

Mark couldn't help feeling just a hint of pleasure and relief. Of course, he wanted Billy to pull but it didn't have to be Sarah. She had brightened up the pub and given him, and the other two, something else to think about other than the shop and Amanda. He knew that Danny felt the same as, earlier in the bogs, he had confessed to having a particularly erotic dream about Sarah, himself and Kathy Bates from the Farm. Mark knew that Billy would mess it up by trying to shaft her on the first night, she would then have to leave and they would be back to Barry's bad moods and Brenda's pilchard rolls and piss stains.

The whole pub was silent as they awaited Sarah's reply. Even Harry Booth the incessant singer from Fagley, who had been humming *Dancing on a Saturday Night* by Barry Blue constantly for the last eleven years, shut up.

Surely, she wouldn't say yes.

Barry had started a book in the taproom and was offering ten to one on against her accepting and was planning to have Billy executed by a professional hit man, Mad Enzo from Girlington, if she did. He knew that he should have insisted on a "Don't go out with any of the regulars" clause in her contract but that would have cost another fifty pence and he had lost the last of his money at the auction, betting on the hamster fights.

What would she say?

Quiz

The Napier had never felt more intelligent.

Ask the Family, *Runaround (turn it in kids)* and *Screen Test* with Michael Rodd. There is nothing like a truly intellectual test to get the brain cells going and quiz night at the Napier certainly did that. Apart from a naked lap dance and poetry recital from Sue Lawley of course. But even that wouldn't have distracted The Three Amigos from tonight's quest for knowledge.

They had been studiously revising for the last two weeks in preparation for the challenge of the educationally subnormal visitors from the Chimp's Arse, a pub in Clayton with an Aboriginal theme throughout.

Billy had put aside his Spanish notes and fervently thrown himself into the influence of baroque furniture design on sixteenth century Gomersal. Danny was now considering studying for a Ph.D. in African cheese and Mark knew all the members of Earth, Wind and Fire, including family histories, convictions and favourite sexual positions.

Tonight, was their last match and they just had to win. Being twentieth out of twenty in the Bradford and District Adult Quiz League would have been funny apart from the fact it was not. The previous team to have come last, the Chimps Arse from Clayton, had only completed half the league due to two of the four team members being certified pathologically insane and the other two had run off to set up an alligator farm in Bangkok.

They had reformed the team after the business had gone bust, a crocodile farm in Shanghai was offering zero per cent finance, and they were now lying in nineteenth place, above the Napier on alphabetical order. To be behind the Arse was a disgrace on par with Sid's record collection, and Barry had even contemplated playing himself in the forthcoming home tie. Luckily, the boys had talked him out of it when he heard that Brenda was making the half-time sandwiches.

Being captain of the team and a degree student, Billy felt the pressure more than the others did. They had lost all of their previous nineteen matches and the knives were out. There had even been talk of a makeshift gallows being erected in the taproom if they lost to the Arse and he didn't want to be remembered as the only man to fight a monkey in a dustbin and not come out on top. Brenda had also promised a top night out at Batley Variety Club if they won, with front row tickets for Reg Varney's jazz funk ensemble, chicken in a basket and a shag from Shirley, cake shop owner and slag, Spencer's daughter, Miranda. This was to be their big night and therefore Billy had decided to cheat.

He knew that the team was weak. He knew a lot about Spanish, football and Spanish football. Danny was brilliant if there was a question on urban warfare conflicts of the twentieth century and Mark was shit hot on fish, fishing and fisheries but that still left a bit of a gap.

Their fourth team member, Tony, who had only got in because his blind dog, Cyclops, had become a bit of a team mascot after bumping into the question master, didn't even know he was in a quiz most of the time and thought the questions were just polite enquiries about the health of his dog. Therefore, he answered every question with "blind", which had worked well in rounds on Stevie Wonder, playing three card brag and Venetian curtains but was fuck all use the rest of the time.

Billy had decided to play a ringer and therefore sacked Tony, and Cyclops, which caused ructions in the local Kennel Club where the dog was a bit of a hero, and approached his Spanish Tutor, Mr Clifford, to play in the team instead.

Mr Clifford was a brilliant scholar and had once won the Turner Prize, a carriage clock donated by Turners of Pudsey, for subliminal use of juxtaposition in a second hand car advert. He had degrees in Spanish, Portuguese, Latvian and a Ph.D. in Medieval Eastern European Literature, which was very handy at Slovakian book fairs. He was also a very shrewd businessman and had invested heavily in anabolic steroids and lesbian videos, making a packet from the East German Women's Athletic Team of the '70s and early '80s. Getting him on their team was a masterstroke and Billy was confident that the evening would end in triumph.

"So where is he?" Danny asked, as the entourage from the Chimps Arse arrived, immediately setting up a transient camp in the car park, with quite an impressive display of Aboriginal guana painting and a masterclass on how to cook emu.

"He said he would be here." Billy looked at his watch nervously. Mr Clifford was already twenty minutes late and the mood of the big crowd in the Napier was already beginning to turn ugly. Tony's dog was giving him a particularly hard stare, which was quite a feat seeing as it had no eyes.

"Well he'd better hurry up as the barmaid is here." Danny pointed to the cowelled stranger, who had just slipped in the side entrance.

The Bradford and District Adult Quiz League was so-called because of the adult content of the questions and also due to the topless barmaid, specially employed to serve drinks during the half-time break.

"Well if he's not here in five minutes, you'll have to ask Tony." Mark added. "But he's crap. We will never win with him in the side."

"But Billy, we can't even start the quiz with only three players and who else can we get?" All three turned and looked around the Green Room, packed to the rafters but with a total I.Q. comparable to that of a Man U fan.

"He'll be here," said Billy, but with less conviction, "he gave his word."

The team from the Arse started to file into the Green Room, leaving a trail of eucalyptus leaves and discarded witchetty grub carcasses. Their team captain, a Betterware man with a boomerang fixation, handed their team sheet to the appointed quizmaster and match referee, Mr Sidney Offal, and they sat down behind the old oak quiz table.

Again, Billy had pulled a fast one. A "clever friend" at college had hacked into the Quiz League computer and inserted Sid's name as match referee. The boys from the Arse had no idea that the man charged with the questions and scoring the match was Sid, the most loyal Napier fan since Ted Malt, a registered epileptic who hadn't missed a Darts and Dominoes fixture for the whole of the 1940s. Billy had subversively been plying Sid with Mild and chips for a whole week and was confident that the Great One would come through.

Sid was taking his role as quizmaster very seriously. Just the previous day he had cashed in his life assurance policy, taken out when Mary used to torture him with knitting needles and crochet hooks, and bought a sparkly jacket from Gratton. He wanted to look sharp and therefore had combed his hair a la Bobby Charlton and slicked it down with Marmite. The girls would love that and he was looking forward to a fulsome tongue caressing his beefy topside sideburns later in the evening.

"So where is he?" asked Danny as Billy, having taken the call, returned to the Green Room.

"He's been caught up." Billy couldn't look at the boys and was now searching desperately for Tony.

Mark whispered as he looked nervously at the tap room boys, beginning to fashion a range of weapons out of darts, sherry glasses and some of Brian Dibble's chest hair. "In what? Barbed wire! A fucking combine harvester! A Portuguese attempt to rubbish the works of Julie Andrews?"

"At a Slovakian book fair." Billy's face was red with both embarrassment and anger. "Apparently he heard that there was an extremely rare eighteenth-century copy of *1001 Things to do with Beetroot and Gypsies* by the great Ivor Bolokov at an impromptu car boot sale in Shelf. And…"

"And he thought sod the poor bastards from the Napier and their impending death by dart. I'll go buy a Romanian cookery book with travelling influences! Nice one Billy." Mark got up to go to the bar, but as he did, the crowd growled. He quickly sat back down.

Danny, who wasn't normally this calm but, on anticipating a good kicking, had taken about twenty Valium before coming out and now passed the cigs around.

"What's the problem? Even with Tony we could beat this lot. Look at them!" He did have a point. The team from the Arse did not inspire intelligence and were currently taking it in turns to groom their captain. "Go on Billy, ask him."

As if by magic, the crowd in the taproom parted like the Red Sea to reveal Tony, and his dog, facing Billy and the boys, a look of anticipation on his face and a dog chew in his hand.

"Ok, but tell him he doesn't have to answer "blind" to every sodding question!"

The deal was done. Tony, having agreed to compensation of a fag and a tin of Bounce for being dropped in the first place, took his seat, Cyclops on lap, and the quiz began. The format was six rounds of questions, each round on a different subject, with each team member having their own question in every round.

To answer it without conferring scored two points. To confer with the rest of the team, scored one point. However, only one attempt per answer was permitted and therefore the team member had to state if they were going to confer before giving any answer. A bonus one point was available if the question was passed over to the other team. After the third round, there was a break for sandwiches and the Beer Round.

"So, at the end of Round One the scores are,
     The Napier, no points, and The Chimps Arse, eight."

Sid had contemplated announcing the scores in Dutch, like Katie Boyle on the Eurovision Song Contest, but had decided against it when he discovered that Holland had invaded Bradford during the Limpet Glut of 1948.

"We were just unlucky, that's all. Who would have guessed that the first round would be on *Aboriginal Homelands of Northern England*? We'll pull it back." Although trying to be, Billy was not so confident having seen Danny fall into a drug-induced stupor and Tony answer "visually challenged" to his question on the staple diet of the West Yorkshire wallaby.

He looked at Sid, trying to catch his eye and get some kind of acknowledgement that things would get better, but Sid was far too wrapped up in his role as quizmaster to notice and was furiously trying to develop a personal catchphrase for use in Round 2.

"Well you'd better be right. Look at Barry." Mark pointed to the bar, where the burly landlord was sharpening his incisor tooth with a rasp.

"And now for Round Two. The subject for this round is *"The Pros and Cons of Reptile Farming"*. It's a fucking laugh, t'int'it?"

"T'int fucking half!!!" the crowd answered. Sid was on to a winner. But it seemed like the boys were not.

When it came to the break at the end of the third round, they were losing twenty-four – two.

Having failed miserably in the round on reptile farming, they had only scored two points on their questions about *Great Australian Rivers* and this was because Tony had been tonguing Cyclops at the time of his question and had simply called out "Darling". Although the crowd had been seething during the quiz and making cut throat motions towards the boys, things were a little quieter now as the Beer Round approached and along with this, the imminent arrival of the topless barmaid.

"Come on Danny, we have to win this," said Billy, trying to rouse Danny from a quite serious coma.

The Beer Round was a single question on the buzzer, with the first team to answer correctly then having a beer bought for each of them by the opposing team. Although they had lost every quiz to date, the boys had never lost the Beer Round, as the thought of having to buy some stranger a drink seemed to wake some latent intelligence in Danny. He had answered questions on topiary, topography and Topov, the monkey from *Pipkins*, and had therefore saved the boys pounds over the quiz season.

"And now Gentlemen, the Beer Round." Sid's sparkly jacket was even more iridescent as he had bribed Brian Dibble, the kinky wireworker from Cleckheaton, to continuously walk round him pointing a torch at his ruby sequins.

"This week's Beer Round question has been selected by Bobby Glover from Bradford Moor. Now sadly, Bobby can't be with us tonight, as he is having a bit of trouble with his wife Peggy. Apparently, last Thursday she was caught getting gangbanged by the Coach and Horse Bar Billiards team after their last gasp victory over the White Bear. Anyway, Bobby is understandably a bit down at the moment so we asked him to pick tonight's question and later I'll be playing his favourite song, *She Bangs* by Ricky Martin. So to Bobby, chin up and thanks for the question, which is,

"Which famous Australian film of the seventies featured a deranged Aborigine and some luscious shots of the bush?"

Danny's hand shot to the buzzer, missed and accidentally poked out Tony's dog's glass eye.

"*Walkabout*" he shouted, as a cheer went up from the gallery.

Only Sid remained calm. "I'm afraid that's wrong. Anyone from the Arse?"

"How do you mean "that's wrong"?" shouted Billy. "The whole film was about getting a glimpse of Jenny Agutter's bush. That was the only decent thing about it. You wait over an hour and then there it is in its hirsute entirety. We have all seen it Sid. You've seen it about forty bleeding times!"

Again, Sid calmly repeated. "Anyone from the Arse?"

It was then that Billy knew he'd been conned. At that precise moment, the light beams from Brian Dibble's torch picked out a range of previous undetected yellow sequins, stitched into Sid's jacket. Put together, these gave the unmistakably spelling of *The Chant of Jimmy Blacksmith*, the answer that the captain of the Arse then calmly gave to Sid.

"That's correct. And the winner of the Beer Round is, the Arse." Sid ducked as Billy launched a pint glass at him.

"Sid, what about the mild and chips you cheating, cretinous bastard?" Billy raged, torn between making a lunge at Sid or a lunge for the door. It was getting really wild in the taproom and the crowd could barely hold their excitement. A topless barmaid and a lynching. Did it get any better than this?

"I haven't the slightest idea what you mean, young man." replied Sid, kicking his five-pound bag of kangaroo steak further under the table and slipping the souvenir Ayres Rock paperweight into his pocket.

And just when it couldn't get any worse, it did.

Sid, who was now being protected from Billy by a group of Hells Angels from the Arse's sister pub, The Gorilla's Testis, had to stand on the table to make his next announcement.

"As this is the last match of the season, the Bradford and District Adult Quiz are proud to announce that the final Beer Round of the season will be for treble shorts and not pints of beer. I know I should have told you that earlier but with all the excitement and the Marmite, I forgot. So lads from the Arse, name your trebles!"

The boys turned to look at each other, as the crowd began stamping their feet in anticipation of the breasts to come. Tony had sneaked off as soon as the Beer Round was announced, leaving a very unhappy dog who had just seen the savings account, opened to pay for laser eye therapy, take a massive hit.

"What are we going to do Billy?" Mark asked.

"Yeah, you got us into this mess; it's up to you to get us out!" Danny had come round very quickly when he found out that he was going to have to buy a treble Bailey's and crème de menthe for the alcoholic itinerant opposite.

Billy thought quickly. Sid could wait until another day.

"When the barmaid comes out, everyone will be distracted and then we make a bolt for the door. Everyone agreed?" The boys nodded.

"And now Gentlemen, it's a fucking laugh t'int'it?" Sid was bang on form. "T'int fucking half!"

"The highlight of tonight's quiz, all the way from Marrakech, its Hot Lea!" Brian Dibble nudged Sid, who was getting far too carried away.

"Sorry lads, make that Mary Ketch from Otley!"

The taproom was in frenzy and didn't notice as the boys slipped down behind the table and made their way across the sticky, rancid floor. And then just as quickly, it all went completely silent.

For a couple of seconds, nobody moved. Then the peace was shattered by the sound of synchronised retching and then emptying of bellies throughout the pub. Vomit splattered the walls, the pool table and the model of Sydney Harbour Bridge, which was made from dead budgies and brought especially by the Arse as a trade for a signed copy of *Tie Me Kangaroo Down Sport* by Saxon.

The boys turned and looked back, first in astonishment and then horror at the sight that had caused this emetic outburst. The lovely naked lady, brought in especially for the evening for her waitress service and pert breasts, was no other than Brenda…

"I knew it wouldn't work without Mark! It has to be all three of us or else it all goes wrong. Sid being the bloody question master! The Chimps Arse! Brenda being topless! Where did all that shit come from?" Danny turned to Billy but he didn't have the answer and was just as pissed off. It was nearly closing time and the two lads were the only ones left in the Green Room.

"I don't know but we created it. I thought winning a quiz would be a brilliant story, especially when we were in last place and in so much trouble. But we made up the Chimps Arse, we made up the stupid, bleeding questions, we put Tony's dog in the team. Maybe you are right. Maybe it does need all three of us to make it work." Billy finished his pint and gathered his jacket from off the Moose horns, stuck on the wall.

"So that's it then." Danny flopped back into his chair. "Mark goes and gets off with the barmaid and we are left sitting in this shithole with nothing to look forward to. It was the same when you took her out."

"How do you mean?" Billy sat back down.

"Well that night you took Sarah to see *The Tin Drum* and tried to shag her behind the Bingo, me and Mark were in here recreating the 1973 Cup Final against Sunderland. Anyway, to cut a long story short, we still bleeding lost and this time both Bremner and Giles got sent off and Montgomery saved a penalty from Alan Clarke in injury time. We didn't say anything to you because you were a bit cheesed off after she knocked you back."

"Danny, it was the same when you took her to the Speedway. We were well into a porn movie with Joan Jett and the blonde one from ABBA, when up pops Olive from *On the Buses* and I'm left gasping at some ginger pubes. It must have to be the three of us."

"Well, that's it then. She has split us up. Mark won't be in a rush to come back, especially if tonight has gone OK. Just you and me in a shit pub talking bollocks. We might as well be Sid!" Danny downed his pint and walked out.

Billy knew that he was upset. Danny had it the worst. A crap job, no prospects and no real opportunity to get out of Bradford. Billy had Spain to look forward to but Danny was stuck in Bradford and was always the most excited of them when the stories came alive.

Things were changing. And quickly.

Romance

"So what would you like?" Mark asked, casually glancing at the menu. Bleeding hell! They charged fifty-five pence for onion rings! These had always come free before!

"I'll have the same as you." She put down the menu and took a large swig of her Mateus Rose. Too big a bleeding swig! It was five pounds a go and they had nearly finished the bottle without even a sniff of the prawn cocktail.

He hated that "I'll just have the same as you" shit. This meant that if he ordered cheap, then she would get cheap and think him cheap. So that meant he had to order expensive, which meant she would get expensive even if she didn't bloody want expensive!

"No, you get what you want. This is a special evening."

Eating out in Bradford has always been one of the better things to do in a city, where entertainment is usually measured by how many pints you can drink before you pass out, vomit and start singing a Smokie song. The choice of restaurants is really quite amazing and on one street in the centre you go restaurant, restaurant, apothecary, pub, restaurant, pub, the Taj Mahal, restaurant, brothel, restaurant, pub, the leaning tower of Pisa, bookies, restaurant, abortion clinic, restaurant, brothel, restaurant, gunsmith, restaurant, pub, taxi firm and restaurant, all within a hundred yards.

Obviously, most of these are curry houses, with the obligatory Formica tables and water fights, where the waiters never lose their temper and you get a treble dose of ring sting on Sunday mornings. Eating curry has almost become a kind of northern induction ceremony to adult life.

Hard men in Bradford are measured on the amount of illegitimate kids they have and their preferred strength of curry.

Shandy lightweights, opt for Korma or Chicken Tikka off the bone with chips and the occasional poppadum. They may spit during a ruck if seriously provoked.

Slightly harder men, who wouldn't mind punching a copper if he deserved it, go for Masala or Madras.

Very hard men, who enjoy ripping the balls off each other, stop at nothing less than Vindaloo and anal sex with prostitutes.

Finally, there is the real psycho nutter, who still thinks Hells Angels and Ivy Tilsley are shit hot, drinks Special Brew with a methadone chaser and goes for Tindaloo, which sticks to their straggly beards and then rots them over the next six months. It is all about bravado and forms part of the learning curve for Bradford youth.

However, there are other places to eat like Cantonese, Greek and Cypriot, and lots of Italians restaurants opened by those who came to the city from Rome in the 1940s after hearing about the gladiatorial battles every Saturday night, free parking and loose women. There was once even an Australian restaurant called The Billabong, which was famed for its flambéed wombat in a XXXX lager sauce, but that had to shut in 1985 due to a spiny anteater shortage in Adelaide.

Mark had to admit that it was a bit of a surprise when Sarah had agreed to go out with him but, after Billy's attempted gropes and Danny's speedway fiasco, he supposed that she was ready for a bit of culture. And that is why he had brought to Bradford's most exclusive restaurant, the Berni Inn on Ivegate. He had contemplated going really upmarket by taking her to Harry Ramsden's in Guiseley, but the smell of fish would have reminded him of Amanda and his certain castration if she ever found out about tonight.

"So why did you come out with me tonight?" Mark was trying to act coy but failing miserably, missing the ashtray and splashing ash all over the nice, white tablecloth, his subsequent attempts to clean this up with his napkin just making a big, brown smudge.

"I don't really know what it is, but you three interest me. Billy is really good looking but is obviously a complete pillock, who for some strange reason thinks that every woman in the world wants to sleep with him…"

Mark nodded, but secretly couldn't see anything wrong with that and, not very secretly, take his eyes off her tits.

"Danny is lovely but it just so bored with life that he doesn't know what to do for the best. I mean, the speedway was a novel idea but Bovril, hot dogs and the bus home! He obviously doesn't really understand women."

Mark casually inhaled, ready to blow the perfect smoke ring. "And me?"

Sarah put down her wine and gazed deeply into his eyes. "Mark, I don't want this to sound insulting, but I really feel sorry for you."

The smoke, that was about to seductively billow forth from his left nostril, suddenly got stuck and then, just as quickly, exploded forth bringing with it a good two and a half inches of purest greenie and a mouthful of Mateus Rose, creating an abstract design on the tablecloth that Picasso would have creamed over. Memories of religious flagellation classes, his pixie dad, his first wife Katie and Danny Goon, the Action Man thief from Trowbridge, all came flooding back. He had spent years fighting against those feelings of inadequacy that come from having a slut mum and a Cornish accent. Granted, he'd married a sabre-toothed bitch but he had built up his own fish and chip empire and won the Pull an Ugly Bird competition on the annual Napier trip. He thought he had progressed.

"You are obviously unhappy with your life and wife or else you wouldn't be in the Napier nearly every night with Billy and Danny, or trying to get me into bed with Mateus Rose and Black Forest gateaux."

"Bollocks!" thought Mark. He had been hoping that she wouldn't want a pudding after her prawn cocktail, T-bone steak, chips and onion rings.

"You are far too clever to be running a backstreet chippy and much too nice to live with that fat cow. So why do you put up with it all?"

He tried to look pensive, but failed, then thoughtful, but failed, so he eventually just took another drag from his cig.

"All three of you need to think about where you are going. Danny is going to end up in prison unless he gets away from here. Billy needs to find some purpose or he'll just drift, turn to drink and end up in the gutter with Sid. And you Mark, she will kill you. What do you really want?"

And that was the ten-thousand-pound question. What did he really want? He knew it wasn't Amanda. She had simply taken over where Katie had left off, although she did have two eyes. He guessed it wasn't even the shop. Although he loved fish and had worked to build up the business, it really pissed him off when customers didn't appreciate the silky white gloss of haddock flesh or the pleasure involved in filleting a particularly difficult cod.

Maybe it was time for a change. His thoughts turned to his dad. News had recently come through, via the squirrels in the forest, that he had turned his back on pixiedom on account of various beatings by jealous gnomes and never getting served in pubs. Hanging up his little golden bell and pointy shoes for the last time, he was now chief exhaust mechanic in Kwik Fit, Taunton and engaged to Dawn, a hairdresser from Wells. Even his mum had stopped hanging around sixth form colleges and was now a high-class hooker on the Dubai circuit. If they could change, then why couldn't he?

"Apart from realising that you are not going to get a shag out of me tonight, what else are you thinking about?"

The prawn cocktail had arrived and Mark gazed adoringly at the plump, pink prawns. They must have come from Morecambe, or possibly that little beach near Skipsea.

"I was thinking... how right you are. For the last five years we have been shutting ourselves away from the real world, pretending our crap lives weren't happening by creating visions in the Napier. We are just too stuck, too apathetic or too scared to do anything else. The Napier provides that little bit of escapism we need to be able to cope with the everyday shit we have to deal with."

"But you are not escaping; you are just avoiding what is real". Sarah reached over and laid her hand over his. "I really like you three and don't want you to destroy yourselves. Working in pubs all these years, I have seen so many sad cases. Men who will sell their back copies of Playboy and Roy of the Rovers just for a glimpse of a barmaid's badges and half a mild. Men who will auction off their distant Estonian cousins to camel herders from Halifax for the price of a bag of dry roasted nuts. Men who will kill for Clan Dew. I seem to spend half my life in pubs helping them to create their own destruction and then the other half putting them back together when I treat them for sclerosis, cut heads and thrush."

Mark knew that things were changing. There was the 1973 FA Cup final debacle the other night in the pub. Billy going down on Olive and then being gangbanged by Jack, Stan and Blakey showed it was getting more and more difficult to create the escapes.

He had also noticed a big change in Billy's behaviour. Whereas he used to simply fluff his way through his course and exams, he had really buckled down to his finals, with vicious rumours of a revision timetable. It was as if he felt this was the time to change things. And Danny's behaviour was getting more and more unpredictable. It was like he was having a permanent period, but without the pale face and big knickers. Mark knew this couldn't go on for much longer.

"So what do you think we should do Oh Wise One of the bedpan and swab?" Mark had started his prawn cocktail and was feeling much more positive, and funny as the fish oils kicked in.

"How the hell should I know? I work in a backstreet boozer and mop up puke most of the day. I just..." Sarah nibbled seductively on a prawn and, although Mark knew this might be one of the great turning points in his life, he still got lobbed up.

Tops.

The waiter, called Mario, but really called Derek and a whippet tester from Odsal Top, hung around on the scrounge pretending to be attentive. People often left grisly bits of steak on their plates, or a stray bit of gammon and pineapple would fall onto the shagpile, and he wanted to get there first before the Albanian chef with the eating disorder.

Testing whippets was an expensive business. Hiring fast children to run away from them and the daily shots of heroin to make their legs shake didn't come cheap. In a way, that's why he had answered the advert in Exchange and Mart and was now Mario, top waiter.

One of his whippets, Alan, had developed a ten pound a day smack habit and, being a humble dog, couldn't really nick televisions or offer backstreet prods to beer bellied desperados from the Napier. Anyway, it wasn't a bad job. This was the era before customer service and waiters actually got bonuses depending on how rude they were. Gobbing in food was obligatory, as was insulting ugly wives and jizzing in omelettes. Only last week he had pissed on Thora Hird as she nibbled garlic bread and got a fifty pence pay rise.

He had been watching the couple in the corner for about two hours. Mario, or Derek, or The Man Who Slashed Over Thora Hird, as he had affectionately become known amongst his fellow waiters and whippet testers, was waiting for his opportunity to screw up their night.

But he didn't need to. The bloke himself was doing a good enough job. Not only had he created a European snot lake, but also had inadvertently knocked an onion ring into his lap, which had amazingly become lodged around his constantly erect penis. Mario, or Derek, or TMWSOTH liked to use adverbs. At this moment, the bloke was trying to whisper sweet nothings into the girl's ear with a mouth full of Black Forest gateau. Not a pretty sight. It looked like he was gargling with Liquorice Allsorts, most of which were being sprayed in her lugs.

"Poor bastard," thought Mario as he flicked his cig ash into the plastic tomato sauce holder in the shape of a plastic tomato and, although it would certainly mean Alan having to go into a detox clinic, he decided to knock a quid off their bill.

"So what are you going to do?" Sarah had cleaned out the chocolate covered cherries from her ears with a toothpick and was now sipping her Irish coffee.

"I really don't know." Mark was feeling slightly sick. His cauliflower cheese had an unusual consistency and a very strong smell and he was about to ask the waiter what kind of cheese they had used, when the brandy arrived. He had passed on the cigar. If a Regal Kingsize could bring forth so much mucus, then a Castella could mean a complete evacuation of his lungs.

"But you have got to do something." Sarah smiled but Mark sensed that her tone had taken on a harder edge.

"I know, but it is easier said than done. I have a responsibility to Amanda even if she is a big fat twat. Plus, I have spent years building up the business, perfecting my curry sauce recipe and persuading Northern inbreds that rock salmon is not actually made of rock. Christ, I even sold calamari once!" Mark could feel his temper rising, nearly as fast as the bile in his stomach.

"Look I appreciate what you are trying to do but you don't really know us. You don't know about Billy's mad parents or Danny's insecurities. You don't know that a man with realistic hair and a Stylophone playing geek from Totnes cuckolded me on my wedding night. Things are easy for you. You can just go to another pub or piss off to Denmark and treat lepers for a while!"

"Mark, I didn't mean to upset you; I just want to try and help."

"But why? Why us? You must have met loads of guys working in pubs even sadder than us. Did you try to change them? Did you con them into buying you a slap-up meal for two without even promising a sniff! Did you tell them to leave their wives, or sort their lives out?" He lit another fag hoping the smoke would take away the acrid taste in his mouth. But it didn't.

"Look, I'd better go," said Sarah, rising from her chair. "I'm sorry if I have said too much. It's just that I know you three are better than all this." Grabbing her bag, she took out three five pounds notes and placed them on the table. "And I wasn't after a free meal." With that, she left, down the stairs, out into Ivegate and past The Old Crown, where the Friday night stripping and fighting was about to commence.

Mario, or Derek, or TMWSOTH looked at the forlorn figure now sat alone, smoking an Embassy Regal king size and swirling the last of his brandy around the impressive balloon glasses that the owner had bought in Skipton market. It wasn't often that Mario felt melancholic. Most of the time he couldn't even spell it but tonight he felt nearly as sad as when his favourite whippet Douglas turned to crack cocaine.

The poor lad opposite was definitely the by-product of a sordid affair between a Cornish pixie and a whore. It was apparent from the way his eyebrows matted slightly. He had married young. Probably a one-eyed girl from Brighton, who promised undying love and then slept with someone else on their wedding night. Clearly, just through his choice of sock colour, he had then opened up a fish and chip shop but again had married a fat arsed cow who beat him up. And finally, it was now evidently obvious that the Albanian chef had once again spunked into the cauliflower cheese as a cornucopia of seventies haute cuisine arced its way across the J B Priestley lounge and splattered the pianist, halfway through his ragtime rendition of *Voodoo Chile*.

Exams

On the same day Bill Foggitt, the aged weather-worker from Yorkshire TV, had found squirrel vomit coating catkins in a misty glade five miles outside Goole. Apparently, this foretold the fall of the Roman Empire, a dodgy consignment of hazelnuts amongst the rodent population of Humberside, Princess Margaret getting a round in and the end of the world.

It was the type of day when you wake up to find an errant pubic hair has somehow got lodged under your foreskin and you know that, if you pull it out, it will be like cheese wire going through your bell end.

Or when your sister beats you to the Frosties box and gets the plastic model of Brigitte Bardot that you have been coveting for weeks.

Or you find out that you slept walked during the night and pissed all over your gran.

Poor Billy. The day of his finals and both his mum and dad had decided to return that very morning. The doctors at the mental hospital, where his dad had been hibernating throughout the rutting season, decided they could do nothing for him and had therefore released him back into the wild.

They had tried various therapeutic techniques such as letting him suckle a baby giraffe and run wild with the jaguar on Ilkley Moor, but nothing had really worked. He had shown a slight improvement when the geese had flown south for winter but since the tadpole season had started, he had nearly suffocated twice trying to breathe through Brillo Pads stuck to his neck like gills. The final straw was when he ate a raw guinea pig.

His mum however was really mental. Suffering from a Toyah fixation, brought on from a particular bad trip during the Iron Maiden tour, she had rainbow dyed her hair, constantly sang shit songs and talked with a lisp. She had arrived in the middle of the night on the back of a Honda Goldwing ridden by Jimmy Page's cousin, Ted, a roadie for thrash metal outfit The Emetics. Apparently, she had kicked her heroin addiction and was now solely reliant on sniffing Ajax, the Dutch football outfit, which made for enjoyable viewing but the constant sound of clogs got on everyone's tits.

"What do you want for breakfast love?" His mum was busy "laying" the table, gyrating her pelvic mound and slopping fanny batter against the Formica top in a black basque and stockings. His dad lapped buffalo milk from his "World's Best Gibbon" bowl.

"Anything Mum, as long as it's quick." Billy was in a rush as the exams were due to start in about an hour and he still had to go through the Spanish translation of "Gordon the Gopher's Big Adventure in Castleford", one of the set books. "Dad, where are my notes?"

Billy wolfed down his mushroom and peanut butter omelette, which was moderately tasty after six years of his dad's regurgitated herring surprise, and jumped on the number seventy-two. He hated buses, especially in winter where groups of poor people got together and coughed up over each other. He usually managed to find a seat upstairs, where he could smoke one Regal after another and hopefully warn off the threat of consumption.

However, to add to his already shit day, the top deck was full and he had to squeeze in on the downstairs back seat between a sweaty butcher with a gangrenous nose and a schoolie in a short skirt and thigh length blue tights. He didn't know whether to get a rabies shot or a hard on but, as the bus bounced down Leeds Road past the Smokie Memorial, his thoughts were on the exam to come.

The gym was packed full of students lining up pens, pencil cases, packets of Polos, souvenir gonks, teddies and action men. Billy looked forlornly down at his Bic pen, lucky stuffed gerbil and scraggy bag of Midget Gems and wished he had spent more time in the exam memorabilia shop.

Students were turning up with all sorts of confidence giving paraphernalia. Harry, who was studying Punjabi literature and pointing for beginners, had a souvenir stuffed kestrel attached to his desk by a souvenir piece of string that had actually been used by Susan Stranks on *Magpie*. He looked very confident.

The ladies from Silsden, halfway through their course on Lesbianism in Modern Day Yorkshire, all had souvenir vibrators in the shape of Alvin Stardust buzzing away on their desks. They all looked really, really confident.

Even his best mate at college, Raymondo Sutcliffe, who was doing a Diploma in the Political Speeches of Old Mr Grace and was absolutely shit at everything, had bought a life-size model of Alan Minter, the '70s boxing hero. He was whistling *The Winner Takes It All* by ABBA and looking extremely confident.

But Billy had revised. He didn't need these false idols and as he sat down, popped a black Midget Gem in his mouth (the best colour by miles) and opened his exam paper, he felt that his sixteen years of studying were now about to come to a very satisfactory conclusion.

The paper seemed to whiz round very quickly and the orgasmic face of Wendy Craig loomed at up at him from question number seven. "Conjugate the subjunctive case of the verb "llasar". Spanish for "to bumlove". She then dribbled black cherry yoghurt into his lap. Suddenly he was floating along on fluffy, white clouds made of Ovaltine froth and blackbird spit, past The Woolpack where a pregnant Amos Brearley waved a white hanky at him and a luminous Mr Wilks shot sheep and rhinos with a spud gun.

"What the fuck is happening?" shouted Billy, as Mike Baldwin mounted the Count of Monte Cristo on a grassy knoll just south of Wetwang and Tom and Jerry played Operation with the cast of Mind Your Language. His head was spinning and his eyes felt like they were being bathed in Asti Spumante, as they tickled and danced in the diamond lights.

"Billy, BILLY! Are you OK?" Raymondo was stood over him as he came to in the canteen. His jeans were covered in spew and his mouth felt like a toad had spunked in it.

"Jesus Christ mate, what the hell are you on?" Raymondo asked as Billy sat up against the canteen wall. "You completely flipped in the exam and had to be dragged out by the Second Eleven Fisting team".

Billy tried to stand up but his legs would not take his weight. "What did I do?"

"First you starting chanting "Amos, Amos, it's my baby",

then you danced like a dad at a wedding to a Mud song, thumbs up and plenty of hip swinging, and finally you projectile vomited over your exam paper before passing out in a state of independence!"

"What about the exam?"

"The exam finished over three hours ago. You have been out of it for ages! And of course, you have failed. Spewing on your paper is not going to get you a pass mark! And naturally, because of your terrible attendance record, the University is never going to pay for your retake and…"

"Just fuck off Raymondo!" Billy reached for the tissue that some kind person had left by the pool of vomit and began to mop his jeans, which smelt terrible. His head was still spinning a little but, through the haze, he could make out the shape of small fungi at various stages of digestion all down his legs. Very small fungi. In fact, mushrooms so small, you could almost believe they had magical properties.

Emmerdale

The rush from the bakery boys was nearly over as Mark mixed up the final bucket of batter for the day. It had been a busy but enjoyable lunchtime as Amanda had decided to take the day off to have her stomach stapled. She had tried various diets over the years, the majority of which involved her getting fatter, uglier and angrier. Mark had once tried to tell her that he would love her no matter her size, but he knew it would be a complete lie so he didn't bother.

He shouldn't be too hard on her as last week she had come up with the idea for fish bits. Half size portions of haddock for pensioners, babies and skint members. These had become unbelievably popular and had been selling out as fast as she could get them from the wholesalers. At first, Mark had been a bit dubious as Amanda's last big money-making scheme was deep fried brisket in a Florentine sauce, served with scraps. Mark knew it was a cardinal sin to serve meat in a fish shop but friendly persuasion in the shape of a kick to the nuts had, for a brief time, helped to change his mind.

"Now then Tony." Although Mark was facing away from him, he knew it was Tony from the loud yelp as his latest blind dog bumped into the hot counter and knocked over a jar of pickled onions. "Usual is it?"

"Cheers Mark, but chuck in an extra Spam fritter for Cyclops. He's had a bad day." Tony, although intellectually challenged in most areas, knew his psychology and that by calling a blind dog "Cyclops" would cheer it up no end.

"What's up? He's not been in the Post Office trying to shag that plastic Guide Dog for the Blind dog again has he?"

"No, she blew him out at Christmas because of his shit present. Bitch! He'd saved up all year for that spice rack!" Tony bent down to pat Cyclops, who was busy playing keepy-uppy with a pickled onion. "No, it's the bloody eye laser clinic! A couple of months ago he'd arranged some cataract treatment at the Yorkshire Clinic. He'd sorted out a BOGOF deal with that short-sighted rabbit from Woodhall Avenue. Booked in, paid up and ready to roll. He'd even organised a sightseeing tour of Wibsey to get the full technicolor benefit. Anyway, it turns out this rabbit had simply forgotten to eat his carrots for a week and now has perfect eyesight again, with poor Cyclops left with having to foot the whole bill. He's gutted."

"Poor lad, it never seems to go right for him." Mark remembered when Tony had bought him a Braille copy of *Lady Chatterley's Lover*. Cyclops was just coming to the dirty bit when he trod on an errant Spiny Anteater who had escaped from the Chimp's Arse. His paws had taken months to heal and, by the time they had, he had forgotten how to read.

"Anyway, talking about bad news, what about the new chippy opening on Woodhall Road? I saw Sid in the Napier and he said they were the best chips he had ever tasted."

Mark knew it would happen one day but he had been hiding the thought away like you would a mad relative or an ugly bird. Another fish and chip shop. Bollocks! Over the last couple of years, he had seen off fast food competition from Mr

Wang's "Suk Yuk House", the Aslam Brothers' "Curry in a Hurry", Big Gay Paul's "Burger Me Bar" and a Lebanese brothel that served complimentary sandwiches with every hand job.

To be honest, he hadn't always played fair. He had bankrupted the Aslam Brothers by sending Amanda and her sister Fiona to the "Eat As Much As You Like" buffet. Big Gay Paul never got over the slur put around about the stickiness of his Mile-High Dressing. The brothel had shut after a visit from Sid.

"Whose shop is it?" asked Mark, trying to keep the nervousness out of his voice. He knew that any sign of anxiety would impact on the quality of his frying.

"I'm not sure." Tony was too engrossed in the sprinkling of vinegar over his crispy batter to notice any lilt in Mark's voice. "Sid mentioned something about a really fit bird working behind the counter but, then again, every bird is fit in Sid's world. He didn't say much as he was on his way to the charcuterie."

Mark began to feel a little uneasy.

"This girl. Did she have a tattoo of a smoked kipper on her left shoulder?"

"I don't know. All Sid said was that she was fit. And… she had a small crescent shaped burn on her left hand."

Now he felt very uneasy.

"Can I have a bread cake and a can of dandelion to go with that Mark. Mark? What's the matter? Mark? Mark! MARK! You are burning Cyclops' fritter you twat! And if he hasn't had enough bad news recently!" Tony slammed his money on the counter in disgust, collected his dinner and left dragging

Cyclops through the vinegar slick on the chip shop floor.

But the young fryer was too far away with the fairies, pixies and halibut to notice. "Why her?" But of course he knew why.

Mark had never been one for affairs. Having to service Amanda once a month took most of his strength, and all of his spunk. In addition, the high level of concentration and dedication required to run a successful chip shop meant he had to keep his mind on fish fillets rather than beef curtains. However, there had been that one occasion where he had strayed, like a lonely yet lovely Dalmatian puppy, whose lead has become untied and seeks adventure in the great expanse of Bradford Moor Park.

It had been on the Bradford and District Fishfriers Annual Dinner Dance in Esholt a couple of years ago. Amanda hadn't been able to make it as one of her thighs had exploded and so, under the threat of castration if he even stood near another woman, he had gone alone.

As was the tradition with the Fishfriers Annual Dance, there was a theme based on where the dance was held. Over the years this had included a "Come As Your Favourite Cheese Night" in Wensleydale, a "Miner's Night" in Barnsley and a "Black and White Minstrel Night in Kingston, Jamaica. Mark knew as soon as he was given the name badge of "Jackie Merrick", and she "Kathy Bates", that their lives would become entangled.

For those of you who don't know, and if that means you, then you should hang your heads in eternal shame, Esholt is where the great *Emmerdale Farm* was originally shot. After buying the obligatory *Emmerdale* snow dome in the Windsor's corner shop, the party had moved to The Woolpack where a full scampi supper was served. The Ephraim Monk's ale had flowed generously, and after winning the prestigious award for Best Battered Sausage and the Harry Ramsden Lifetime Achievement Award for Services to Pineapple Fritters, Mark was on an all-time high.

He had noticed her first when playing bar billiards with Ma Sugden. She was different from most of the women there. For a start, she didn't smell of lard and her hair wasn't matted with the accumulated years of chip fat. Then there was the tattoo. Mark marvelled at the simplicity, yet the beauty of the kipper design that adorned her shoulder. He had last seen a fish like that on the quayside at Filey in 1978, a beautiful bloater that he had craved but unfortunately not been able to afford. He had thought about it for weeks and masturbated continuously, remembering its silky brown flesh and superb bone structure.

And, as she turned to face him, all those happy memories came flooding back. Her skin glowed like a freshly filleted turbot. Her body, much less than a size twenty, flowed through the amassed throng like a mature salmon and she even had two eyes. He simply had to have her.

The evening passed quickly and, although he constantly tried to engage her in conversation, he seemed to be steered by others into conversations about the optimum temperature for frying fish cakes and plastic fork suppliers. But then, as the final dance approached, *We're having a Gang Bang* by Black Lace, he found himself next to her, taking in the heady perfume of Givency's *Mystic Cod*.

Without speaking, she fell into his arms and they

smooched away whilst the rest of the Fish Fryers simulated group sex around the dance floor. Her name was Marina and she ran a small shop just outside Ossett. The Woolpack emptied around them as the music ceased and landlord began collecting glasses and the little white polystyrene trays that the buffet had been served on. Mark had never felt such sexual tension since a particularly tight skate one July in Scarborough and, as she collected her coat, his thoughts were definitely not on going back to Amanda and her exploding leg.

"Look Marina. I know we have only just met but…" She placed one finger over his lips to quieten him and then guided him towards the edge of Esholt village.

"Where are we going?" asked a puzzled Mark as she led him around the back of a row of terraced houses.

"You will see." Marina answered quietly. She then picked up a small brick and gently smashed open the glass partition of the back door on the last of the terraces. "I know Joe Sugden is away working for NY Estates, so Demdyke Cottage is free tonight," she said, reaching in to turn the key and open the door.

Fuelled by the evening's mackerel canapés and the fact that the girl under him had both eyes, didn't sweat gallons or explode in a fishy orgasm, Mark made love like there was no tomorrow. His body, freed of the eighteen stone of flesh that he usually tried to deal with, became like a conger eel; lithe, supple and in an out as fast as a Scouse in a power cut. They both came together under an Emmerdale moon, as foxes bounded playfully, owls swooped and Seth Armstrong poached rabbits off Holme Farm.

"When will I see you again?" she asked, held in his arms.

Mark suddenly felt a little uneasy, a bit like Jim Bowen when he first presented *Bullseye*.

"I'm not sure. I know that next year the annual dance will be held in Cape Town, where we will be all party to the filleting of a Blue Marlin. I would love to see you there."

Suddenly Marina pulled away from him sharply and he felt a little dribble of sperm cascade down his thigh. Not a bad feeling though as Amanda usually pissed all over him. But he could tell that Marina wasn't happy as she got out of the bed and began dressing herself very quickly.

"So that is it? We share bodily fluids and the best way to chip King Edwards and then you just blow me off like some cheap rent boy from Manningham Park. What is it, Mark?"

"Things are too complicated at the moment. My wife would kill both you and me if she knew about this and I'm sure you are aware of the proposed fishing quotas in German Bight." Mark had been worried about this for weeks as he couldn't even speak German but Marina didn't even seem to be listening.

"You bastards are all the same. First there was the burger van magnate from Shelf. Thought he could ply me with ketchup and stories of Aberdeen Angus, shag me and then dump me for Auntie Bessie, just because she made half decent Yorkshires. He got it."

Mark was now getting worried. He had read in the *Telegraph and Argus* about the supposed suicide of Wilf Langran, suspiciously found drowned in a puddle of batter with a fillet steak on his heart.

"And do you remember the Pizza shop owner from Morley? Thought he could sniff oregano off my flaps and then abandon me for a hairy-arm-pitted waitress from Bologna. Marina's face was now redder than an infected foreskin, as she gathered up her bag and packets of tartar sauce.

"It was so sad to hear about him being found dead, quartered by a pizza cutter with pepperoni slices over his eyes. But don't you worry Mark. I have much sicker plans for you." And with that she was gone, leaving Mark in Demdyke Cottage, afraid and alone just like when Archie died as the plane came down, leaving a blind Nick Bates wandering across the moors of Beckindale, bumping into sheep.

And now, two years later, she had returned. Apparently not to kill him but to close his shop with her expert chipping and the best curry sauce recipe since Hare Krishna had first started experimenting with cumin and fenugreek. Mark knew that the sad, old regulars like Sid and Tony, and the boys from the bakery, would desert him for her winning smile, her fantastic knockers and the fact she could sell lemon sole to even the most dubious of fish eaters.

Mark didn't hear Amanda come in the shop to get her lunchtime daily bucket of mushy pies and twelve breadcakes. Obviously, they couldn't have found a big enough staple. He knew that all he had ever worked for was now about to melt as quickly as a snowflake in Elland.

Sacked

Danny knew that he was in trouble as soon as he saw the rats deserting the factory and heading south to Mr Azaq's carpet emporium on Leeds Road. They had always stuck by him in the past, even having a whip round to buy him a travel iron for his week's holiday in Tossa de Mar. But it seemed like this time that they knew the writing was on the bog wall. And to cap it all, Andy, his long-time partner in grime, had also sided with the management on this one.

Standing outside Mr Tally's office looking at a signed photo of Jack Wild during his *H. R. Puffinstuff* years, he thought of what H would say, what his mum would do and if he would go down for this one. He remembered when Larry Barker had come out of Armley jail after a two-month stretch for decking Tufty the Squirrel during a road safety demonstration. He had gone in a hard man, full of Bradford bravado and with enough strut to impress even the cockiest cock. Eight weeks later even Sid felt hard enough to call him Marjorie and flick ash in his beer.

"Get in here now!" shouted Tally, as Danny contemplated doing a runner but changed his mind as the heavens opened. He didn't have a coat. He walked into the office, expecting to see Tally at his desk but was surprised to see him stood at the window. That could only mean one thing and, as Danny turned to Tally's desk, there he was.

"So Danny, you have finally crossed that line that shouldn't be crossed." The smell of Gitanes was very strong, as was Swarfega, and the voice was deep and resonant like a bronchial Orson Welles. Danny's eyes adjusted to the smoky haze and fell upon Old Man Radebe himself, specially flown in from his semi-retirement barge in Suez for the imminent sacking.

Danny noticed a difference from the last time he had seen him, which was at his dad's funeral. The lime green Gola tracksuit and matching trainers had gone, replaced by an expensive copy of a C&A double-breasted. The hair was the same though, defiantly black and slicked back with otter grease, as were the eyes, hard and piercing like a fucked-off budgie.

"Tally says this has been coming for years and that you have had more second chances than Frank Bruno," mumbled Old Man Radebe, as he picked up a glass of Tizer. Billy noticed his personnel file open on the table, along with a Kung Fu death star and the evidence from his latest escapade. Old Man Radebe took another drag on his Gitanes and let the smoke waft towards Danny, creating a scene from some World War II Nazi interrogation.

"Do you know, Danny, that I have spent the last forty years trying to create a better life for the people of Bradford? People said I was mad to carry on with this engineering factory in the arse-end of the world. Hitler wanted me to run his munitions factory in Dresden. Stalin offered me millions to make fancy wrought iron gates for the Kremlin in an impoverished town just outside Minsk. Fuck me, I was even offered the contract for the aluminium smelting plant in

Warrington. All those recycled pop cans sent in by sad, misguided Blue Peter fans, thinking they were helping spackers. Just think of all the weapons I could have made with those! And yet I stayed here to Bradford. And do you know why?" The jet-black eyes now focussed on Danny, suddenly making him feel very cold, as the bitter November rain pounded against the office window.

"No, I don't know why, but I'm sure you have made plenty of money out of all of us, Old Man. My dad died paying for your exotic lifestyle. The trips to Suez, the designer shell-suits and those fucking awful French fags you smoke." Danny suddenly forgot the cold, as the anger from ten year's frustration rose in him. "What exactly have you done for us? The factory is an asbestos dump, the wages mean that half the men in the fitting plant have to pimp their daughters to the Arabs in Undercliffe and I am still here, making fucking missile parts with Thompson and that cunt Tally!"

"You, cheeky little bastard," shouted Tally, moving forward to grab Danny but he was too quick and lashed out, knocking the factory manager to the floor.

"Enough Danny," hissed Old Man Radebe. "Tally, go and get Nurse Mary to clean you up. I can handle this." Tally left the office, blood streaming from his nose and his bent finger now even more bent than a Larry Grayson tribute act.

"Sit down Danny." Old Man Radebe gestured towards the chair in front of Tally's desk. Danny slumped down and lit a Regal King Size.

"So are you going to sack me or what because *Blue Peter* starts in twenty minutes and I so love to wank over *Janet Ellis?*"

Old Man Radebe smiled, his dark forehead revealing white wrinkles that had been masked by fifty years of accumulated grease and camel dust.

"You still are the irrelevant little sod that I first set eyes ten years ago. Of course I am going to sack you. Engraving "Reagan is a Wanker" into fifty missile heads bound for the US forces has cost me a couple of million pounds, Tally and Thompson their jobs, and the probable closure of Plant One, which will make you about as popular with the Asian workforce as Salman Rushdie eating a pork chop. But first I am going to tell you a story. So just shut the fuck up for a few minutes and listen." Old Man Radebe lit another Gitanes and began...

"Times were hard in the forties. Britain was at war with the Germans, the Japanese and the Welsh for non-payment of being English subs and too much community singing. But it made real men. Men who were prepared to die for their beliefs, their king and so they wouldn't have to explain to their wives where the fuck they had been for the last five years.

"I had been running a brothel in Cairo when I first met your dad. He was a captain in Montgomery's Desert Gerbils, and had fought across the whole of North Africa, bayoneting Algerians in the Tangiers conflict, blowing up Libyans on the feast of Stephen and kicking the shit out of Moroccans simply because it was fun.

"The Desert Gerbils had arrived in Cairo when Montgomery had decided it was time for a bit of R and R. He had caught syphilis from a belly dancer in Alexandria and wanted time off to pass it on to the bitch's daughter, a supply teacher showing errant French chefs how to make couscous.

"But after ten days of haggling over carpets and being ripped off about maps, supposedly showing where Tutankhamen had buried his papyrus prints of Cleopatra taking it up the arse, the Desert Gerbils were getting a bit lary and had therefore decided to arrange a ruck with the fans of Cairo's top firm, the Nefertiti City Crew. Nefertiti City had once beaten Bradford Park Avenue in the 1938 Random Cities Cup Final and, as you know, your dad had once been the Avenue's top striker. Obviously being brought up in Helsinki, I was top man in the NCC and therefore it was all arranged to kick off at sundown, behind the Pyramids of Giza."

"What the fuck has this got to do with anything, Old Man?" asked Danny, who had the attention span of a gnat with an OCD. "Time is getting on so just sack me and then I can get to the job centre before it closes. You never know, there might be a job for an unemployed rebel without a clue."

"For once in your life, just listen. This is important." Old Man Radebe began again.

"It was a good ruck. Proper fist fight and not a Stanley knife, meat cleaver or Kung Fu Death Star in sight. The NCC were putting up a good showing, even though we were outnumbered and our desert sandals were no match for the Gerbil's hobnailed boots. After about ten minutes, I got separated from the rest of the crew and found myself getting a savage battering from about ten of the Gerbils. I thought my time had come as they took turns kicking me in the head, the balls, everywhere.

"But then suddenly they stopped and, as I peered through the blood pouring from my head, I saw your father. He kneeled down and offered me some water and a rag to clean myself up, before calling for a jeep to take me to the hospital. I spent three days there before my balls had shrunk enough that I was able to walk again. I had asked at the hospital about the man who had sent me here and I finally got the name of your father. I swore on that day that I would always look after the man who had saved my life."

"Look after! My dad died from working in your fucking diseased factory," retorted Danny. "If it wasn't for you, and your greed, and your fucking shell-suits, he might still be alive!" Danny was now standing and pointing angrily at Old Man Radebe.

"I know how bitter you are Danny, but please let me explain," calmly replied Old Man Radebe.

"During the war, I had made millions from my string of brothels, selling sand to the Arabs and getting a very good price on pomegranates from the Isle of Lesbos and that's why I came to Bradford. To find your dad and make sure that I could repay my debt to him. I set up the engineering plant, got a great contract making canisters of DDT so the Yanks could burn the shit out of the Vietcong and then found your dad. I asked him to be a partner in the firm and that we would split everything fifty/fifty."

"You lying bastard!" Danny was apoplectic with rage. "We have never seen a penny from your success, just crappy wages paid and a couple of shit Christmas bonuses."

"I know that's how it seems. But your dad was a very proud Scot. He believed in a fair day's work for a fair day's pay and refused my offer point-blank. I tried to convince him but he just wanted to be left alone and simply get on with his job. He didn't want the responsibility, the Gola shell-suits or the villa in Morecambe. Believe me Danny, it's true. If not, then just ask H."

Danny's head was in a whirl. "What do you mean just ask H? How do you know H?"

"Danny, my boy, H has done jobs for me all over the world. He brokered the deal when Radebe Engineering built the Panama Canal. He negotiated the contract to rebuild Budapest after the revolution in Hungary and he personally auditioned Linda Lovelace when Radebe Films made *Deepthroat*. H tried on many occasions to persuade your dad to change his mind but he was a stubborn sod and refused again and again."

Danny collapsed into the chair opposite the Old Man. His whole life had lost any meaning. He thought about the times they had struggled, how he had to leave school at sixteen to work in the factory to boost the family income and how his dad, and mum, had suffered when he was dying. And, it all could have been so different.

"Don't blame your dad. He was a proud man and I admire him for that. And he wanted the same for you. To work hard, get a trade and live an honest life. But you and him are very different."

Danny didn't know what to think and what to say, so simply leant over the desk, took one of the Gitanes and lit it up, the blue acrid smoke driving straight into his lungs.

"And now I need to sack you. The only reason you are still here is because your dad asked me to give you another chance. And I did, on many occasions, when others would have been in jail or taken out by the NCC. But this is not the end Danny. Speak to H when you can. It will all become clearer then. Now go, before Tally raises a lynch mob for your guts."

And with that, Old Man Radebe slipped out of the back door, leaving Danny alone with his torment and unemployed status.

Sad

The Napier had never been as solemn.

It is always sad when good things come to an end. Like when David Bowie killed off Ziggy Stardust and simply became another cockney wanker in a blue suit. Or when they cancelled the eagerly anticipated third series of Fawlty Towers because Basil had accidently bullied Manuel to death. Or when they stopped making Arctic Rolls and all we had for pudding were Vienettas.

And now, the Napier was also dealing with its own heartache. Shirley Spencer, cake shop owner and slag, was dead.

After literally days of fruitless searching the globe for a new strain of plankton, the whelks in Shirley's tits had eaten all her pancreas and had started nibbling away at her bowels and bladder, leaving her permanently incontinent.

Brenda, being the kind soul she was, but not wanting to splash out any more of the SOBs coffers on a revolutionary treatment from Syria, which involved replacing the whelks in her tits with attentive stag beetles, had tried simply standing her in a bucket of Domestos in the corner of the taproom and hoping the smell would go away, but it didn't really work.

The Darts team lost five games on the trot, as the stench kept putting off Brian Dibble, the kinky wireworker from Cleckheaton, from hitting his world famous double twenty-one. Tony's blind dog kept bumping into the bucket and knocking it over leading to evacuations of the taproom on par with Dunkirk and or being duped into seeing Genesis live. Even Sid, a taproom regular since Moses had got pubes, was now frequenting the Keith Mumby suite, fucking off all the regulars in there with his tales of when Bradford ruled China.

Things finally came to a head during the annual Gordon Burns Night celebrations in June (the Napier regulars had always loved the Krypton Factor although they had no clue what was going on), when Barry had been piping in the traditional Corned Beef Hash. Somebody had discarded half an inch of still lit Old Holborn on the taproom floor, igniting the heady mixture of Shirley's methane and flaming Sambuca on the hash. It wasn't a pretty sight and, as the smoke cleared revealing a lot of scorched hair and a dead blind dog, Shirley's chargrilled body was devoid of life.

Brenda was absolutely distraught. She and Shirley had been through a lot together; the darts and dominoes team from the Adelphi, the pool team from the High Flyer and the British Lions rugby squad during a training camp in Horsforth. Shirley was her best friend, she collected Brenda's fishing maggots every Saturday from the Halal butcher on Darley Street and Brenda had been there when Shirley's daughter, Miranda, had been expelled from school for interracial porn. So she was determined to give Shirley a proper send off.

The open casket in the taproom had been a mistake though. Shirley's still smouldering carcass was not a pretty sight, especially as the now famished whelks were hurriedly abandoning the body and heading for the cheese plant in the Green Room. Only the bravest of the brave filed past the coffin, well the big saucepan, and threw in the customary pork scratching.

To cheer herself up, Brenda had immediately booked a two-week trip, tiger shark fishing off Australia's Gold Coast, and was currently in conversations with the Queensland Fisheries Commission to see if Shirley's remains could be used as chum. It was what she would have wanted.

Barry had also been a bit down recently. Although he had never cared for Shirley, she had once shat on his knee when he had been conned into playing Father Christmas, he knew that this would hit Brenda hard and that he would be expected to console her. Just the other night she had asked for a hug. Last night she had demanded a goodnight kiss to stem her aching heart. If this carried on, by next week she would be expecting arse sex, which with Brenda's explosive rectum would leave him traumatised for weeks.

He was also beginning to question his own mortality. He had worked really hard, well moderately hard, well worked to turn the Napier into the less than adequate drinking establishment that it had become. But as he scanned the lunchtime drinkers, all dressed to the tees in their finest charity shop serge suit combos to commemorate Shirley's passing, he asked himself if it was really worth it.

What a fucking motley crew...

Tommy, who had once read a book, had taken it upon himself to perform Shirley's eulogy and was currently reciting an extract from Ian Fleming's "The Man with the Golden Gun", creating a very tenuous metaphor between Scaramanga's third nipple and Shirley's emaciated knockers to the expectant taproom regulars.

Brian Dibble, the kinky wireworker from Cleckheaton, had brought his wife to the wake, Doris Dibble, the despotic dinner lady from Dewsbury, and she was getting on everyone's tits by forcing the masses to get into orderly queues while they waited for their fish finger and fairy cake buffet. Barry had never met her before but he now knew why Brian spent so much time in the Napier. The poor bastard.

Tony, and his new, but not yet blind dog, Roy Orbison, (Cyclops had gone in the explosion that had killed Shirley as he was drinking from her bucket at the time), were doing an impromptu demonstration of arc welding without face masks in the car park. When would Tony ever learn?

And Sid.

Barry had recently begun to warm towards Sid. Not like you would warm towards a recently discovered long-lost relative, who was unfortunately from Wales, but had a sack full of cash, a pan of faggots and a mint Tom Jones collection.

But Sid was a compass of degradation that Barry could measure himself against and as long as he remained north of Sid's Michael Barrymore impression, then he knew that he had a good chance of purgatory.

However, even after all those kindish thoughts, Barry was going to have to bar him. Sid had turned up to the funeral dressed as Majid the Motorway Mongoose, believing that the get together today was to teach the infant Pakistani population of Bradford Moor how to dodge unlicensed taxis on Leeds Road.

Sarah was also feeling the strain.

She had been working at the Napier for over six months and it was beginning to wear her down. Although she had got used to the crudely written messages on beer mats asking her for two-pound hand jobs, and Sid's constant reminders of his love for her by playing "Sarah" by Fleetwood Mac on the jukebox every bleeding night, she had realised it was time to move on.

She had applied for a job mending poorly kids in the Costa Rican rainforests and being the only one person in the whole wide world who had been remotely interested in it, she had got it. Apparently, the village youth were all addicted to licking green tree frogs and ending up with bad stomachs and mad hallucinations. This meant they were fucking useless at hunting howler monkeys and so the local village elders, in fear of their tribe going extinct through starvation, had put an advert in the Bradford Telegraph & Argus, hoping to find their very own Dr Quinn, medicine woman.

There was also the fact that The Three Amigos, her only respite from the usual panting and salivating customers, were hardly coming in anymore.

She had seen Mark a few times but he had been very sheepish since the meal out. Danny had told her about the projectile vomiting of the cauliflower cheese, adding that Mark had shit himself four times as well, although he later admitted to making that bit up for more comic effect, and so she could understand why he had been embarrassed to chat with her at the bar.

Danny himself had become very distant since his sacking and hardly spoke to anyone. His just sat by himself in the corner of the Green Room, chain smoking Gitanes for some reason. Barry had nearly barred him the other night for lamping Larry Barker over a heated discussion on which one of Charlie's Angels was the fittest but, because it was Larry, he decided to let Danny off and gave him a free pint instead.

And Billy, since messing up his exams, had not been in at all.

Sarah was dreading telling Barry and Brenda. The pub was still, at best, a shithole but takings had gone up since she started, the number of fights had reduced dramatically and Sid didn't stink of piss half as much as he used to. She knew that she had made a big difference to the Napier but she had to let them know soon. The village elders were already in the process of building her a straw hut and slaughtering a tapir for her welcome feast.

But not today. Not at Shirley's wake.

"What will it be Brian?" asked Sarah, reaching for a pint glass, as Mad Alf Reeday, dressed as a fat and nearly dead Elvis, broke into his version of *There is a light that will never go out* by the Smiths in the Green Room.

Followed with *Fire* by the Crazy World of Arthur Brown.

And ending with *Shirley's Saggy Tits*, a tribute song that he had penned himself.

Casino

Billy didn't need to open the letter from college to know that he had failed his exams. That had been obvious from the moment he had eaten the fungi surprise created by his mum, who had once again disappeared. According to Mrs Senior, the nosey neighbour from ninety-nine, Billy Idol had turned up the other Tuesday on a Harley Davidson, a rucksack full of coke and two tickets for Marbella and she had just nicked off like that, disappearing quicker than Paul Michael Glaser from our TV screens after Starsky and Hutch was cancelled, leaving Billy and his dad alone again.

Not that his dad had even realised she was gone. He had totally wrapped himself in clingfilm, and was simply laid comatose on the sofa, believing himself to be in the chrysalis stage of the Great Hawkdown moth. Billy could only be sure that he was alive when he wiggled a bit during Animal Magic but anyway, he had more urgent things to worry about.

As Raymondo had so tactfully alluded to during his vomit smothered comedown after the exam, the letter had confirmed that he would no longer be getting a student grant, his attendance was worse than an Auschwitz commandant at a Nuremberg trial, and that it would cost him two grand to re-sit his exams.

Two fucking grand! Billy didn't have anywhere near that kind of money. He knew his dad had blown all his pension on

139

a stuffed Kodiak bear that he played Ludo with on Wednesdays, and the only cash his mum ever had went on gin, bingo and speed. He thought about Mark but he knew the chip shop wasn't doing great at the moment and Danny was always skint, especially now he had lost his job.

Billy tried to call Alan, Danny's brother. He sometimes had a good tip for the horses, he had bought his house in Yeadon after picking the first five in the 1983 Cheltenham Gold Cup but then shown what an utter twat he was by naming his sons Bregawn and Silver Buck (Captain John and Ashley House were also in the top five). Anyway, his phone was dead as Yeadon had been under curfew since Christmas, when the whole town had rioted due to the planned Government cuts in public stonings.

There was only one thing for it. Casino.

Although Bradford in the '80s still made living in downtown Beirut look glamorous, it did have one casino. It was in the cellar of Bradford's only three-star hotel, The Norfolk Gardens, and was rumoured to be quite a classy place. Billy had never been but he had seen many a tuxedoed gent slipping in the side door after a boxing event at the hotel or when Big Daddy was bouncing into Giant Haystacks at St George's Hall.

Billy had never been a big gambler. Of course, he had played brag at school, and lost a few quid on the weekly cock fights in the sixth form lounge but the only time he really had had a bet big was when playing strip poker with the Tidgewell Triplets but that had just been a frequent, but brilliant, wet dream.

But things were desperate and so Billy went to the college

140

library (a first) and got out a book on how to win at blackjack. He withdrew the last one hundred pounds from his post office account, opened to pay for his new life in Spain. And, because he didn't have a tuxedo, he borrowed his dad's white jacket, bought when he needed camouflage in the winter to stop the polar bears that frequented Bradford Moor Park from eating him. Billy then booked a Thornbury taxi to take him to the casino.

Although he hadn't been expecting Casino Royale, Billy was shocked at how down market the level of clientele actually was. He saw a few familiar faces from college, trying to bolster their student grants, that annoying double-glazing salesman, who kept trying to convince his dad that UPVC windows would attract a better species of fruit bat, and Dot Cotton from EastEnders. There were also loads of Chinese people, who you never actually saw on the streets of Bradford during daylight hours, but who were now swarming around the gaming tables as if there were free insects on sticks on offer.

Billy felt a little let down, instantly regretting the white jacket as a pissed-up Carol Vorderman sloshed her red wine across his sleeve. But the one thing that did catch Billy's eye were the girl croupiers.

God they were all fit, made up like professional models and dressed in very tight and very revealing light blue evening gowns, obviously wearing thongs or, even better, nothing underneath. Billy couldn't take his eyes off them. He hadn't seen as much crumpet since the conveyor belt in plant one at the bakery had jammed. It was only the sound of a familiar voice that disturbed his reverie.

"Hi Billy. What are you doing here?"

Billy looked for the source of the voice and saw to his absolute shock that it was Seven Up, or Alan Mitchell, the physics geek from school. But a very different Alan Mitchell. Gone were the blue plastic framed National Health glasses and the crinkly perm that everyone had taken the piss out of for years. Contact lenses, a smart short haircut, a bit like that of the Smiths bassist, a full dinner jacket with black dicky bow and a badge on the lapel reading "Alan, Casino Manager", all showing that this was indeed a very different Alan Mitchell.

"Wow Seven, sorry Alan, you look like you are doing OK." Billy was pleased to see a familiar face but slightly narked at how successful he looked, and he had also never really forgiven him for deflowering Jane.

Alan moved out of the casino pit and towards Billy. "Come on, let's go for a drink and catch up" he said, ushering a nervous Billy towards a very expensive looking bar.

But Billy didn't need to worry about the cost of the drinks as Alan simply nodded to the barman each time their glasses of expensive Dutch lager needed refilling. He started to relax, as they swapped old school stories, both purposely avoiding Jane and, of course, Katie Marsden, although Billy had to hold himself back when one of the croupiers loudly announced "Seven, Red", the colour of Alan's face for three months after his moment with Katie.

Billy finally got onto the debacle with his exams, his two grand shortfall and thus the reason for him being here with his hundred quid. Alan had listened intently throughout but now shook his head.

"Let me tell you now that you are not going to win two grand tonight. If you are lucky, you will only lose fifty. If you are very lucky, you will break even. If you have the extreme luck of an Irishman, who finds a four-headed clover and the pot of gold at the end of the rainbow, then you might win a hundred quid."

Billy could see that he was being both serious and honest with him.

Alan continued. "I have been working here for three years and have seen loads of bright-eyed punters, convinced they can beat the casino. Card counters, people with mathematically designed systems to read the roulette wheel, we even had a so-called witch doctor from Little Horton perform an exorcism over the punto banco table. It always ends the same. What starts off as a fun Saturday night out inevitably ends with either divorce, suicide or assassination by Mad Enzo of Girlington for non-repayment of extortionate loans. If you are really serious about getting your two grand together, then why not come and work here?"

Billy, who had been getting more and more down listening to Alan, suddenly perked up.

"What do you mean? I am not qualified or anything," Billy replied, but with eagerness in his voice that betrayed his misgivings.

Alan smiled. "Not a problem Billy. Each new recruitment campaign is simple and the same; a fit blond, a fit brunette, a fit redhead if we can find one, a fit girl from a different ethnic background, a good looking lad who keeps the grey brigade happy and an average looking lad, who can actually do the job. You would be the good-looking lad. I'm doing the interviews so you are nailed on if you want it."

Billy looked over at one of the roulette tables, where a

young Italian looking croupier was being leered at by a group of very old, and very ugly Jewish women, and immediately remembered his encounter with Brenda in the Napier cellar

"But you don't have to do anything with them, do you?" asked Billy nervously, seeing the poor croupier being pawed by the diamond encrusted hand of an octogenarian with brown skin as tough and leathery as a rhino's arse.

"No, it's against company policy. You just need to smile and make them think they have a chance," replied Alan, a big grin on his face. "We have a training school starting next week. It is working nights, but the money is good, and I'm sure it won't take you long to save the two grand. What do you think?"

Billy took another hard look at the beautiful brunette dealing blackjack. She had the body of Cindy Crawford but a dispassionate air about her, like a young Siouxie Sioux.

"But it's OK to see the other croupiers?" asked Billy.

"Oh yes." replied Alan, an even bigger grin on his face.

Football

"So are you in Danny?" Hooligan's enthusiasm could only be matched by that of a teenage boy, who wakes up one morning and discovers what his cock is really for.

Danny looked up from his VDU. "Who's going?" he asked.

"Me, you, Gadger, Angry Chris, you know the guy from IT called Chris who is always angry and Hatter, if Luton aren't playing and we don't drink too much. It's going to be fucking great. We've got calling cards, great seats near the away fans and don't forget but you need a parka."

"Why do I need a parka Hooligan, it's the middle of bastard August?" Danny asked incredulously.

"Because we are the Parka Service Crew, the famous PSC, and that's what we wear." beamed Hooligan and then disappeared as fast as he had arrived to tell the others.

Danny had to admit he was enjoying his new job.

He had seen the advert on his first visit to the job centre after the sacking. He wasn't in the best of moods after Old Man Radebe's revelations and expected the job centre to be just as depressing. And he wasn't disappointed. Danny was reminded of the Band Aid video that had gotten everybody so upset, you know the one with all the precocious twats pissing around in a recording studio, pretending they cared about dying Africans, whilst drinking Starbucks coffee.

However, there was a job working in a call centre for a tool hire company in Leeds and, because of his engineering background, and a total lack of previous employment checks, he had flown through the interview and was now in his third week.

The money was OK, the hours were fine and he was meeting new people, which was important now that Billy had virtually disappeared working nights and Mark was in so much trouble.

Because it was based in Leeds, most of the lads who worked on the phones, or in the supply warehouse, were massive Leeds fans. Although born and raised in Bradford, Danny had always been a Leeds supporter, mainly to piss off most of his schoolmates, who were all Bradford City, but also it was because of his dad. He had been a great friend of the late Bobby Collins, the Scottish midfielder, who captained Leeds in the '60s.

And so with that, Danny became one of the original members of the PSC.

A week later, dressed in the green fish-tailed parka that he got from C&A, Danny entered the Dragon pub on Gelderd Road, about half a mile from the Leeds stadium, with his new PSC mates; Gadger, the laid back but always hungry one, Chris the angry one and Hooligan the excitable one. Hatter hadn't made it as they had decided to meet in a pub.

"So Hooligan, please can you tell me why we are in the pub four hours before kick-off?" asked Gadger as the three of them sat down, while Angry Chris went to the bar to get four pints of Fosters.

"Simple. It's so we can have about eight pints and still get to the ground with a couple of hours to go, get the best seats and have a pop at the away fans" replied Hooligan, his excitement undeterred by the sarcastic lilt in Gadger's question.

Danny smiled as he responded. "But Hooligan, we have season tickets and therefore get the same seat every game. We don't need to rush to get in. And anyway, we are playing Bournemouth and they will only bring about one hundred fans."

Leeds had been languishing in the second division for about ten years and, although things off the pitch were looking up a little, the PSC could still look forward to less than sexy games against the likes of Plymouth, Oldham and Shrewsbury.

Angry Chris came back from the bar. "For fuck's sake, please tell me he is not going on about fighting the away fans again. Hooligan, I have told you a hundred times, we are not a real firm. We are not going to fight anyone. This is just a bit of fun."

Hooligan's grin faded for a second but then returned just as quickly. "Yes, but the away fans don't know that." Danny couldn't help laughing and realised that, for the first time in ages, he was really enjoying himself.

Gadger picked up the tatty Dragon menu, stating, "Well if we are going to be here in this shithole for another couple of hours, then I'm getting something to eat," promptly ordering the impressive sounding pork stack. Gadger was the biggest carnivore since the extinction of the sabre-toothed tiger and on a recent stag do in Prague had dined on zebra, crocodile, wildebeest and some pygmy goat.

After a couple of hours, and a tremendous bout of the meat

sweats, the PSC set off for the stadium, stopping only when Angry Chris angrily aimed a kick at a passing car that had nearly run over his foot. He then nearly started a fight with the driver, a nervous and sobbing eighteen-year-old thalidomide girl, who had just passed her test and was having trouble parallel parking her invalid car in the busy thoroughfare.

Once inside the ground, the PSC sat back in their seats, lit fags and looked forward to some of the best football ever.

But it never happened.

Both Leeds and Bournemouth were terrible, even though it was the first game of the season, the ground nearly full and you would have thought that they wanted to impress. The only bit of entertainment in the first half came when a deflected shot from Leeds striker, Bobby Davision, hit the post and Hooligan, in his excitement of nearly seeing a goal, jumped up and accidently lobbed his still lit Embassy No One about three rows in front into the hood of the only Chinese Leeds fan in the ground. The PSC then waited expectantly to see if his coat would catch fire. But it sadly didn't.

After about thirty-five minutes into the game, Gadger suggested adjourning to the season ticket holders bar, as he had seen they were selling Chicken Balti pies. They all agreed and filed out of their seats, all except Hooligan who was determined to see a goal, and they never went back, preferring to spend the second half drinking shit lager and joining the other pissed up Leeds faithful in many renditions of the Runway song.

And so began the legend of the PSC. And Danny loved it all.

The season didn't improve and the football was so bad

that the boys got later and later in turning up to the ground and then earlier and earlier going to the season ticket bar. For the Shrewsbury game, they turned up half an hour late, after drinking cheap bottles of rose wine in the Dragon to celebrate Gadger's birthday, went to their seats in the South Stand and then left for the bar five minutes later when Ian Baird missed a penalty, the only real attempt at goal in the game.

Their unattendance at games was building the PSC's notoriety and causing much amusement amongst the other supporters who sat around them; the two Irish lads, who weren't Irish but Nepalese, Mick from Bramley, who had no teeth but sold great speed to the infants at Wortley Junior School, Seether One and Seether Two, who both just constantly shouted "fuck off" at the ref throughout the game and the google-eyed, but big-titted Amy, who sat behind the PSC, and whom Angry Chris had shagged in the toilets during a particularly tedious nil – nil draw with Swindon.

In fact, Ladbrokes stopped taking bets on the first Leeds goal scorer and made millions with spread bets on what time the PSC would arrive and leave.

"So Danny, what do you reckon to Preston away?" Hooligan was now resigned to the fact that the PSC would never get into a ruck at Elland Road as they were either too pissed or not even there, and was therefore seeking new adventures.

Danny had never been to an away game with Leeds and was slightly nervous. It was well known that the proper Leeds firm, the Service Crew, always travelled in big numbers to away games, and he was a bit worried as one of them had been nicked and sent down for throwing one of his kung fu death stars at a copper.

But what the hell.

"Fine but I am not wearing my parka." replied Danny, who had been sick down his after a stupid bet to eat a cricket ball sized marzipan egg had gone horribly wrong during the Ipswich game.

It is absolutely true that, when Charles Dickens penned his famous novel "Hard Times", he based the filthy, industrial metropolis of 'Coketown' on Preston after he visited a group of striking cotton workers there in 1854.

And fuck all has changed. Apart from the fact that Charles Dickens is dead.

People from Preston will say we gave you Tom Finney, some old footballer in long shorts and a centre parting no doubt, the man who played R2-D2 in Star Wars, I'm about to come, and Nick Park, the creator of Wallace and Gromit, those hilarious plasticine characters who always mess up the Boxing Day TV schedule.

"Preston actually makes Bradford look good." agreed Danny proudly, as their train pulled into the station.

The journey there on the train had been good natured, full of Leeds supporters in their club colours enjoying a few cans of Fosters and games of brag. Danny felt relaxed among this crowd but had noticed that the few transport police on the train were closely watching a gang of about thirty fans at the end of the carriage, all dressed in Fila, Ellesse and Pringle sweaters. These were obviously the Service Crew and Hooligan got very excited, begging them to move down towards that end of the train. A quick kick on the shins from Angry Chris soon stopped him.

After a short, but exciting bus ride to the ground, flanked by a police motorbike escort, and a few choruses of "Tommy Finney is shit, his wife's a slag", Danny and the PSC were herded into the ground and took their seats in the away end.

But once again, the football was crap and, after Leeds conceded a second goal five minutes into the second half, Gadger suggested leaving and trying to catch the earlier train back to Leeds. The stewards, seeing that they were only four of them, let the boys out and the PSC began the twenty-minute walk back to the station.

They were just about to turn into Station Street when a black police van suddenly screeched to a halt beside them and six burly officers jumped out of the back.

"Where the fuck are you lot going?" barked the sergeant in front, wielding his truncheon menacingly.

Hooligan, who was very excited at finally getting some action, was just about to make a witty retort, when Danny jumped in. He had heard about the fearsome reputation of the Lancashire Constabulary. They had once pepper sprayed Bobby Charlton for his comb over and gangbanged Bet Lynch for wearing too much leopard skin print. And they weren't over-fond of Yorkshire people either.

"We are just going back to the station to get an earlier train." said Danny calmly.

"No, you are not. You are coming with us." And with that, the PSC were escorted by the six policemen to a very rundown looking pub about fifty yards from the station, with its entrance surrounded by another thirty uniformed policemen.

"You can stay in there with the other Yorkshire yobs until

your train arrives" said the Sergeant, directing them to go in the pub.

The pub itself was like any other pub you find near a train station in any town; old-fashioned, filthy and only selling one brand of bitter, which had been in the cellar for two hundred years and had the consistency of thrush discharge.

"I suppose any food will be out of the question." said Gadger, gloomily, but the others weren't listening as, at the other end of the pub, there were about twenty of the lads that they had seen earlier on the train. But these lads had a different reason for leaving the ground early.

They had briefly looked up when the PSC entered but, on seeing only four anxious Leeds fans in shit parkas, they had simply carried on drinking their pints, snorting cocaine off the pool table and hatching devious plans to escape the police and cause mayhem. Hooligan was beside himself and Angry Chris had to bribe him with Dutch porn to not go over and introduce himself.

It seemed like forever as the PSC nursed their pints and waited for their train but, about an hour later, the doors burst open and about twenty policemen barged into the pub, ordering them all to leave their pints and exit the pub. The PSC promptly got up and made their way to the door, followed much more slowly by the Service Crew boys. Danny had a feeling that something was going to happen, as the Service Crew were all whispering to each other as they filed outside, but he soon forgot about that when he saw what was waiting for them.

Although the station was only fifty yards away, there were about two hundred policemen lining either side of the street, obviously to stop the Service Crew from going anywhere but the station. Danny had to admit that it felt pretty special to warrant such a reception and he could see the other PSC boys smiling, obviously thinking the same.

The procession continued peacefully towards the station. It was clear to Danny that the Service Crew boys were used to this special treatment as they were nonplussed by all the attention, even swapping casual insults with the policemen lining the streets.

Then suddenly, probably after an insult too far, or perhaps the start of a bigger plan, one of the Service Crew aimed a roundhouse kick at a policeman's head, knocking him to the ground. Almost immediately, the police broke ranks and jumped on the lad. Seeing their chance to escape the cordon, the rest of the Service Crew then scattered in all directions, leaving the PSC in the middle of the street, surrounded by truncheon wielding pissed off coppers.

Danny wasn't sure whether to run or stand still. He looked for the others and saw that Hooligan was now bounding away, following a couple of the Service Crew, as excited as Merlin the Happy Pig, but he couldn't see the others. Fights were breaking out everywhere and Danny decided he had better get out of there, remembering he was still on a suspended sentence for the incident with the kung fu death stars.

He saw a gap in the police lines and made a bolt for it. But just as he was turning into a quiet side street, he felt a vicious blow to the back of his head. And then, nothing.

"Wake up, you fucking Leeds scum. That will teach you to mess with the Lancashire Constabulary."

Danny couldn't see who had spoken but roused himself

and discovered he was in a small cell with a massive headache and quite a lot of blood on his shirt.

"Don't worry, you are not dying." He could now see a desk sergeant, peering at him through the bars.

"You Leeds wankers are all the same. Think you can come to this lovely town and attack our brave policemen. Well you are going down for this my lad. You have one phone call so you had better make sure that you use it wisely."

Although his head was still foggy, Danny knew it was time to ring H.

Bankrupt

Mark rested on the chip shop counter during a very quiet lunchtime opening and reflected on his predicament.

"Bittersweet," he surmised, faintly pleased with himself for the choice of an oxymoron after contemplating the whole range of his current thoughts and emotions; delirious, in the shit, cheerful, miserable, free, crippled, happy, skint, safe, worried-sick, positive, negative, lucky, despondent, timely, depressed, delighted and totally fucked up.

His musings were ended by the sound of the bell on the door and Tom from the bakery came in. "Relieved" quickly concluded Mark, as Tom always put a big order in for the Saturday lads working there.

"Afternoon Tom. I've got the haddock battered and ready to fry. Usual order is it?" asked Mark, expectantly.

Tom should have been Welsh, he looked so sheepish, his eyes focussed on the floor and his voice as shaky as Michael Parkinson with Parkinsons.

"I'm sorry Mark but I just popped in to cancel the order." he mumbled, almost incoherently.

Mark slumped back against the wall, knocking the jar of pickled eggs off the shelf and hearing it smash on the floor.

"Not you lot as well?" he replied, trying to hide the sound of desperation in his voice. "Why now Tom? You have been coming here for three years now and I have never heard a complaint. I even give you a free can of Dandelion and Burdock for picking up the order."

"Well, you know. The Saturday lads are young and like to try new things and…"

"Don't tell me," interrupted Mark, "they have heard about the marvellous new curry sauce and the brioche bread cakes and want to give it a try!"

"I'm sorry Mark. It's not me." said Tom.

And with that he left, looking as awkward as a female secondary school biology teacher, who is calmly trying to explain the facts of life and then gets asked by the class clown what 'lobbed up' means.

Mark looked despondently at the ten or so pickled eggs, wobbling like weebles around the wet tiles of the shop, and tried not to get upset. But that really was it. If the bakery boys were now going to Marina's, then his only regular customers would be the desperate Mums, on their way home from work, who had forgotten to take the burgers out of the freezer that morning.

First there had been Sid and, although he only ordered small chips and a battered sausage, he'd had that every day for the last eight years and it all added up in the weekly takings. Apparently, he had been converted by her Pineapple Fritter Loyalty Scheme, which promised a free day trip to Flamingo Land after the five thousandth fritter, although Sid was convinced that Flamingo Land was in Tanzania, where he believed his long term pen pal, Kunta Kinte, lived.

He didn't.

And Sid couldn't write.

Then Tony and his now blind dog, Roy Orbison, had been

tempted by her deep fried Bonio biscuits, a simple but brilliant concept that had now been endorsed by Crufts.

And now the bakery boys, entranced by her sweet buns and masala inspired curry sauce.

Mark had to admit she was excellent at marketing and, although he had always been a bit if a purist at heart when it came to fish and chips, focusing on the quality of his beef dripping and freshness of the fish fillets, he had to admit that the age of exotic accompaniments was upon them and he had to change.

The shop's bank balance said the same.

Since Marina had opened "Frivolous Frying" on Woodhall Road, Mark had seen his takings drop by nearly fifty per cent and he was now getting into quite serious debt with the bank. He had walked past her shop on a number of occasions, jealous of the queues outside, longer than that of a Latvian bread counter that has just received a consignment of mouldy baps. He had even seen her in the shop, her tight fish fryers apron barely covering her ample breasts and the small tattoo, which he had gently caressed during their one night together, openly on display.

He had thought about popping in to say hello and see what reaction he would get, but he was too wary of Amanda and what she might do to his nuts if she ever found out.

But then he grinned, suddenly remembering what was sweet about feeling bittersweet.

Mark had woken up a week ago with the strangest feeling.

Firstly, he didn't have cramps in his legs. He was usually stricken with chronic pins and needles for about half an hour each morning as Amanda always draped her gargantuan thighs across him during the night in case he thought about sneaking out and shagging someone else.

And secondly, his cock, usually limp and flaccid like an African baby, was firm and upright.

He looked across the bed, expecting to see the vast expanse of her mottled white flesh snoring away until feeding time at twelve, but instead saw to his amazement, and relief, that it was empty.

He dressed quickly and went downstairs. Usually if Amanda was up at this time then it meant that she was hungry and Mark was worried that she might be wading into his ever deplenishing stock. But the shop was empty.

Mark was confused. The last time Amanda had disappeared was when she and her sister had heard about a two for one offer on Steak and Kidney pies at Yates' Wine Lodge in town. She had come home two days later, bloated with pastry and sicking up gravy. But she hadn't mentioned anything, usually unable to contain her excitement at a cheap meal.

It was then that Mark saw the note on the kitchen table, crudely written on a napkin using about a hundred sachets of tomato sauce that he sold in the shop.

"Dear Mark,

Sorry but I have got to go. I saw the bank statement and know that you are skint. I cannot live with you thinking about where the next meal will come from. Me and my sister are off to live in Munich, where apparently there are giant sausages. Not like yours, if you get what I mean. Shag anyone else though and I will come back and kill you.

Luv Amanda"

Mark didn't know what to think.

He supposed that he had loved, well liked her once. She had soulful eyes like Bambi's when his Mam was shot, and she could be very gentle and loving, especially after Sunday tea when they had salmon sandwiches and Mr Kipling's Manor House cake and watched Bullseye together.

But then he remembered the frequent beatings, the mood swings when Mr Abdul's corner shop ran out of Manor House cake, the tantrum when the couple from Halifax won the fucking useless speedboat on Bullseye and, most horribly, the monthly retching when she forced him to try the beard on.

He had thought about leaving, even getting rid of her a few times, once in a drunken state inquiring about the price of Mad Enzo from Girlington, but the timing was never right. There was always another fish delivery to sort or the chipper needed mending. Only last month he had also sought H's advice about leaving her, when they had discussing the plight of the shop, but H always said the same thing. He had to make the decision for himself.

But now it seemed that the decision had been made for him.

He began to scoop up the pickled eggs from the floor, a tricky task as they wouldn't fall down, and thought about how Marina might react if he attempted to make contact. But then the postman arrived, delivering a final demand for the electricity bill, and with Amanda gone, and his genitals safe for the short term, he asked himself,

"What was there left to lose?"

Bottom

"I can only come if it is my arse."

Billy, sat in the casino staff room on his break, choked on his coffee. He was getting used to the racy chat amongst the various dealers but this had broken new boundaries. He turned to look at the source of the explicit revelation.

It was Kate, the casino's top blackjack dealer, an extremely beautiful young Shirley Bassey lookalike, whom Billy had admired from across the casino floor but never had yet found the bottle to talk to yet. She usually worked a different shift pattern to him, so their paths rarely crossed, and she was rumoured to be going out with a professional footballer. So what could he say to her?

But Billy's mind raced thinking about her, especially with what she had just shared with everyone.

He had only tried anal sex a couple of times and, to be honest, he hadn't really got into it. Quite literally.

The first time had been with the daughter of the chemist, where he normally bought his condoms. This meant he never got invited to any of her family parties, or even to her house, although he felt it was quite a responsible thing to do. With AIDS and world famine and all that, but Billy acknowledged that her dad probably didn't like him, especially after he bought a twelve pack from the shop to celebrate his daughter's birthday.

He had been seeing the chemist's daughter for a few months whilst at college but she wasn't really his type. She was very fair skinned and had ginger hair and therefore ginger pubes, which Billy found as distasteful as a Man U injury time winner. But she was always flush, subbing him for a few nights in the Napier with him being a student, and always ready for sex.

Billy had been fascinated with trying anal sex since Danny had borrowed a video off his brother Alan called "Hot Tuna Sandwich", although they were both still unsure where the tuna came in.

She finally agreed, simply to shut him up begging her for it every week, but when it came to actually doing it, Billy faltered at the sight of the two bouncy, snow white globes that lay on the bed before him. He was reminded too much of Bob Todd and the other little bald chap from the Benny Hill show and went as limp as Tiny Tim in a Christmas Carol. They had tried it a few times since but the Benny Hill theme tune always came into his head and, when he started patting her bum cheeks like Benny did to the little one's head, they decided to give it a miss.

The only other time was with Wendy does Wyke, after a really heavy session in the Napier, but her arse was so big that he would have needed a car jack to get anywhere near. And so he had still never done it.

"Come on Billy, break is over" said Nicky, his new best mate from the casino and, awoken from his quite arousing thoughts about Kate and her sexual preferences, Billy went downstairs to the casino floor to deal roulette.

He had been there for a couple of months and was really

enjoying the lifestyle. It had taken a few weeks to get used to working nights but everyone was friendly and he was making a lot of tips that would go towards his exam resit and subsequent life in Spain.

Although he had never realised it before, he was a natural at flirting with the rich, old women that came in every night. They would swarm around his table, spending loads and giving him extravagant tips just because he gave them a cheeky smile or said how glamorous they looked. Nicky had given him the nickname "GILF Hunter" and would often be seen in the background with a mop and bucket, trying to wind Billy up as he dealt.

Nicky had been at the casino for years but his irreverent attitude to both the punters and the casino management meant that he had never been promoted beyond being a dealer. He was always in trouble for some prank or comment he would make to a customer and had nearly been sacked just last week for sprinkling cheese on the seat of a Chinese woman, whose takeaway had been shut down the week before after a mouse had been found in the Chow Mein.

But Billy really liked Nicky as he had taken him under his wing and helped him become a really good roulette dealer. Plus, Nicky lived in the staff house.

The staff house was a big old terrace with about six bedrooms just outside a village called Idle in Bradford. It was owned by the casino and they subsidised the rent so the staff could get rooms very cheaply in comparison to other places in the area. But, best of all, it had a bar in the cellar. Working mostly nights, the casino staff missed out on the normal Friday and Saturday nights out in pubs and bars around town. So the cellar bar meant they could unwind after work and have a more normal social life.

But it was anything but normal.

Nicky told Billy tales of wild parties, almost every night after work, where a few casual drinks would turn into all day drinking sessions and, because both male and female dealers lived there, numerous wild sex orgies that would make a Roman Emperor blush. And Billy had to believe him as Nicky always turned up to work at nine half-pissed or half asleep. Usually both.

He had invited Billy back to the house a few times after work but he'd always had to get home to look after his dad. Being at work all night usually meant his dad needed feeding when he got home, as he now believed himself to be a panda cub and therefore needed fresh bamboo every couple of hours. Billy had come home the other morning to find him devouring loads of wicker shit in the living room and therefore had to go to the garden centre to get a few canes for him to nibble on. Billy was getting more and more frustrated with both his dad, who now only spoke Cantonese, and the social services, who said they wouldn't find him a care home until China gave us Hong Kong back.

But this weekend would be different as his dad had been invited to Scotland by the warders of Edinburgh zoo to join the mating programme for their female giant panda, Barbara Streisand, and so Billy was free.

Because it was a Saturday, the casino had shut at two a.m. and therefore most of the night shift, about twenty of them, had gone back to the house and were all now crammed into the small, but well stocked cellar bar. The music was loud and joints were constantly being passed around, making the atmosphere both heady and relaxed.

Billy nursed a bottle of Becks in the corner. He still felt a bit of an outsider as many of them had worked there for years, and he didn't know them that well socially, but there was no escaping Nicky.

"Now Christine," he said, putting his arm around one of the older, but still very attractive casino waitresses. "Young Billy here has never been to staff party before and doesn't really believe that we all end up shagging each other. I want you to put him right."

Christine slid right up to Billy and let her hand wander across his chest, then down his stomach and finally across the flies in his jeans. She then leant her mouth to his ear and whispered, "I'm going to murder you later," before moving away towards the bar.

Nicky stood grinning at Billy. "I told you, didn't I? You are well in there, she's fucked everyone in the casino, and seeing as it your first party, then you can have my room."

Billy wasn't sure to say thank you or what. Christine was lovely but he wasn't sure if she, or Nicky, was just having a laugh. Nicky sensed Billy's awkwardness.

"Look Billy. Just get pissed and enjoy yourself and what shit happens will happen. You can't spend all night looking like the only virgin in the brothel." he added, almost poetically.

And so he did, joining in the round of tequila slammers, a big mistake, the pool competition, the flaming sambucas, an even bigger mistake, and chatting to a few of the girls there. He was having a great time but then he noticed that Kate had arrived, wearing a very tight pair of leather trousers that

164

seemed to have been sprayed on and, to confound his lust even more, she was with her identical twin sister, also dressed in tight leather pants. He immediately thought of her revelation the other night in the casino staff room and quickly slid a cushion across his lap.

She hadn't been working that night, so must have come after the Cloud Nine nightclub had closed. Nicky had told him about the fabled twin sister, who worked on the perfume counter at Lewis's in Leeds, mentioning that there had been rumours of sibling lesbian love. But then again, Nicky had told him that the Queen and Princess Margaret were also known to drink from the furry cup.

Billy watched them from the other side of the cellar. They seemed very close, as Kate had her arm around her sister's shoulders, but there didn't seem to be any other indication of potential lesbian activity. But now Billy had other things to think about.

He'd been drinking now for about six hours and, after a round of a Nicky inspired cocktail called the Lion Sock, his head was spinning faster than a Battling Top, it's all in the wrist action.

Billy recognised the signs of an impending hurl and therefore, to save himself the embarrassment of vomiting in front of his new friends, and getting the nickname Chuck Two, Chuck One was a croupier called Steve, who had once been sick into the spinning roulette wheel whilst dealing, pebble dashing the entire throng of Jewish ladies at his table in a multi-coloured and multi-textured gloss finish, he gave a quick wave to Nicky and made his way upstairs to the bedroom. He then just crashed on the bed, any thoughts of anal sex, or even lesbian sex, just a distant, but pleasant memory.

Just like every episode of Roald Dahl's *Tales of the Unexpected*, Billy really didn't have a clue what had happened that night. He had woken up, his mouth as dry as a pensioner's fanny, to find himself in the middle of two very beautiful, and two very naked twins, but then had immediately passed out again. When he awoke again, they were gone. He knew it hadn't been a dream as Nicky had confirmed they had slept in his bed, but he had no idea if anything had transpired.

He hadn't really seen Kate since at work and when he had, she had simply acknowledged him with a smile. But now, about six weeks after the night in question, he'd been given a note from Alan to meet her before work tomorrow at the Queens, the pub next door to the casino. His mind went into overdrive. Perhaps they had done it and now she obviously wanted more?

Billy arrived at the pub very early to down a couple of pints before she arrived, just so he was at his suavist, although that was never going to happen. Kate arrived about an hour later, got a glass of wine and sat down at the small table opposite Billy. She immediately began.

"Billy, before you get any ideas. No, we didn't do anything. You are a nice guy but not my type and anyway, I'm engaged to a footballer called Ryan, who has just got a transfer to Manchester United, so I will be leaving soon."

Billy felt his heart being ripped out of him quicker than an Aztec warrior at Chichen Itza. Fucking Man United! Kate continued.

"But there is something. That night you did sleep with my sister Julie and, to cut a long story short, she is pregnant."

Billy gasped, trying to take in what he had just heard. He wasn't sure how to feel. Shocked at the devastating news. Pissed off because he couldn't remember any of the finer details. Or proud that he had still managed to perform after all the booze he'd had. He tried to speak but found he couldn't. So Kate carried on.

"Obviously, she is really shocked as she thought she couldn't get pregnant and therefore wants to keep the baby. And, before you ask Billy, it is yours as she hasn't slept with another man for over three years. She normally prefers girls."

After briefly, but very explicitly, imagining her and Kate getting it on together, Billy finally managed to say something, although he perhaps should have kept his mouth shut. "Does she want to get married or anything?"

"For fucks sake Billy, of course not. She can't even really remember what you look like! Look, here's what she has suggested. If you want to play a part in the baby's life, then you can but you will need to pay towards it. If not, then give her three thousand now, so she can get through the pregnancy, and you will never hear from her again."

Billy sat back and lit a fag. Three grand, would take all the money he had saved for his re-sits, and more. Spain was getting further and further away. It might as well be fucking Pluto.

Billy wasn't sure what to say, or do, apart from to get in touch with H. He would have the answer.

Wedding

The Napier had never looked better.

Apart from its opening day, of course, when Sir Isaac Newton pulled forth the first frothy pint of ale and then immediately declared it the worst pub in the world.

Barry had always felt this a little harsh, especially when the entire population of Finland had been wiped out in The High Flyer after sampling their tripe and cow heel lasagne. And, if he was honest, which he wasn't often, but when he was, he would have to admit that he had played up to this reputation over the years. In fact, Barry had asked Tommy, he who had once read a book, to write a short advertising pamphlet on the Napier's troubled past, with the catchy headline,

"You might have it rough, but nowhere is as bad as the Napier"

Included were those historic moments that had added to the Napier's reputation as a complete shithole; the abolition of rational thought in 1923, the rise of consumption, Keith Chegwin, the Limpet Glut of 1948 and Brenda's attempt at pubic topiary.

In an entrepreneurial moment, matched only when he decided to buy a box of Mini Cheddars from Archie Shag, Barry had then sent thousands of copies to the people of Vietnam, Biafra and Manchester. It had been a huge marketing success and to this very day the Napier still received visits from African famine victims and a commemorative Christmas canister of napalm from Ho Chi Minh City.

Nobody cared about what happened in Manchester.

But Barry had really splashed out this time. He wanted to ensure H's wedding reception went well. Barry had known H all his life and it had been H who had talked him out of joining the Bramley Hitler Youth Movement in the '60s when he had got into leather shorts and goose stepping.

Therefore, he had paid a real painter and decorator to spruce up the Napier. In fact, it was the very person who had restored St Basil's Basilica in Red Square, Fagley, that tarted up the Green Room in a zucchini white and then varnished the urinals in the men's bogs.

Now the pub was spotless, especially after Barry barred Brian Dibble, the kinky wireworker form Cleckheaton, who was covered in spots after competing at the World Chase the Ace Championships in Bangalore.

Barry's renovations had also extended to a complete overhaul of the jukebox, the first one since the great Englebert Humperdink debate. He had scraped out the dead cat and removed the 78s, including an original copy of *Where Have All the Boot Boys Gone?* by Slaughter and the Dogs. He felt uneasy riding into town as he remembered the last time that he had been tempted to update the jukebox too much Wham had got Brenda gushing and the Napier was flooded for a week.

Well, according to Sid, Barry had come up trumps, which was slightly worrying to the other ninety-nine point nine per cent of the entire population of the world, but his choice of German electro pop was going down a storm and he even contemplated contacting the brewery to see if he could order some more Das Deutscher Piss.

H lit one of his King Edwards as he sat back and watched his daughter Susan, and her new husband Keith, begin the dancing. He wasn't a bad lad and H knew that he would take care of her after he was gone.

He felt very tired, but to see those who really mattered to him having a good time was worth all those tours of the Far East, the sweaty Bedouin tents and mule rides through the Colombian rainforests. His whole life had been about sacrifices and helping others. If people only knew about his counselling sessions with Castro just before the Bay of Pigs, or when he had managed to persuade Che not to pose for the 1957 Embassy Cigarette Card collection. Who would've thought that the photo H had taken of him outside the bingo hall in Caracas would have become so famous and made H so rich?

Many of those who criticised him for being away, forgot that he had put up with Mao's mad rhetoric for two years before convincing him it would be better to write it down in a little red book. Or that he had been to Berlin with JFK, tiptoed through the tulips with Tiny Tim and deciphered Martin Luther's dream.

He took a sip of the de Rothschild '74, a beautiful claret with a hint of sarsaparilla, bought especially for the wedding, and raised his glass to Billy, who was teaching Maria, his new Spanish wife, to pogo. He was still an idiot but H couldn't help feeling proud.

He refilled Mark's glass with the excellent wine. Mark

had been sat next to him throughout the ceremony as Marina, his new partner, was in Whitby negotiating a big turbot deal, but at the moment he was swapping business cards with Richard Branson in the Paul Reaney banqueting hall. H made a mental note to charge Mark for the introduction but knew that he never would. Seeing Mark shot of the fat bitch was reward enough.

The only sad thing was that Danny wasn't here. H knew that Eddie, Danny's dad, would have been so proud to see him done up in tails like the other two. As would his mum, sat chatting to Joe Strummer in the Bobby Ham lounge.

"How's your dad Billy?" asked H as Billy slumped into the chair next to him, sweating profusely after a ten-minute Jive Bunny punk mega mix. His wife Maria, completely bemused by the whole punk genre, still managed to crack an extremely beautiful Latin smile.

"He's fine H. I have got him a place in a wildlife sanctuary just outside Valencia. He loves it, mixing with the geckos and wild pigs and has even started hand rearing a colony of meerkats in an old pedalo that he found on the beach. The warders look after him, giving him tapas and Kitekat for the meerkat kittens, as well as giving him his weekly rabies shot after he French kissed that deranged marmoset, Julio, in Alicante.

"Shame about your mum though Billy." H filled up their glasses. "Being locked up in that Chinese prison cannot be helping her career as a Valerie Singleton impersonator."

"No H, she has stopped that now. Too many people were asking her about Jason the cat's gingivitis problems and bumming sticky back plastic from her on the bus. She's now back to her Toyah impression, which is going down a storm in a number of jails."

Billy lit a Fortuna, just one of the little changes H had noticed since he had been in Spain. "In fact, she's about to begin a three-month tour of Cambodian penitentiaries, before moving on to Burma, Korea and a farewell performance in Barnsley's correctional institute for shoplifting mums. She then goes back to China to serve out her sentence proper."

H turned to Maria. "And you my dear, how are you coping with this immature but very bronzed and happy young fool, who has surprised us all by settling down and becoming a respectable member of Seville society?"

"I am very happy and proud." Maria replied, "Billy is now being asked to be the headmaster of the school and all the children think he is wonderful."

H raised his eyebrows at Billy in mock disbelief. "So the kids think you are wonderful do they Billy the Kid? What are you doing? Teaching them to play blackjack and then taking all their pesetas off them to buy your precocious fags?"

Billy smiled. "No, just teaching them to be responsible young adults and not go around the world causing trouble or drinking too much precocious red wine. Anyway H, I just want to say thank you for sorting the money out for the exams and the issue with, you know, the casino times. I couldn't have done it without you."

"You don't need to thank me Billy, because it wasn't me." And with that, H picked up his glass of wine and joined the massed throng, all swaying to a Blow Monkeys medley, leaving Billy shocked and silenced at the table.

At that moment, Mark joined them with a smile as broad

as a Supervixens cleavage.

"Hi Maria. Billy you will never guess. Richard fucking Branson has only agreed to market our Katsu curry sauce! Apparently, fish and chips are massive in Japan and he is going to launch it as part of his Virgin World Food range. He is also looking to open his first sushi restaurant in Bradford and wants me and Marina to manage it. We are going to be millionaires!" But Mark could see that Billy had not heard a word and was simply staring at his wine glass. "Billy what's wrong?"

Maria also turned to look at Billy. "What's wrong beautiful?" she gently whispered.

Billy slowly looked up and beckoned Mark to sit down.

"Mark, you know you told me about when Amanda left, and how H had helped you through it by supporting the shop until you and Marina got together and opened "The Best Plaice". What did H actually do?"

Mark sat down and lit an Embassy Regal king size, his face only seconds before beaming with pleasure, now quite sombre.

"Billy, H did nothing. A few weeks ago, I tried to thank him for getting rid of Amanda and give him a cheque for the five grand that he paid to stave off my bankruptcy but he said he had nothing to do with it." Mark shook his head, as if confused. "I then just assumed that Marina must have paid off the debt, when we got together."

"And did she?" asked Billy.

"To be honest, I have never asked her. All I know is that, when I went to the bank, my debts had been cleared. I then just assumed Amanda went because of the giant sausages in Munich. Why are you asking?" said Mark.

Billy turned to Maria and asked her if she wouldn't mind getting him a pint from the bar. He waited until she left and then spoke quietly.

"Well I thought it was H who had sorted the money for the baby and then paid for my resits. But he says not. I know it wasn't any of the family as they didn't even know about Julie and the pregnancy. It must have been H as he was the only one, apart from you, that I had told."

Mark looked up towards the Bobby Ham lounge and said, "Well why don't we ask him again?" as H sauntered towards them, obviously unable to keep up with the smooth moves required in *Digging Your Scene,* a Blow Monkeys classic.

H sat down and, anticipating that he was about to be hit with a barrage of questions, calmly said, with a massive smile spreading across his face, "Look gentlemen. If you want to know who your benefactor is, then look no further."

The boys followed his gaze to the Napier's main entrance and there, in a very smart blue Armani suit, and with a very tanned Sarah in tow, stood Danny.

The boys stared incredulously for a few seconds but then both jumped up from their seats and, with the normal Bradford protocol of firm handshakes completely forgotten, began hugging their third amigo.

"What the fuck Danny!" exclaimed Mark, acknowledging Sarah with a sheepish smile. "We thought you were..."

Danny gave a nod towards H, who smiled back proudly, and then interrupted Mark, saying,

"Look there's plenty of time to discuss what's been happening. Billy, where is Maria?"

Billy pointed to his wife at the bar, at that moment being

encouraged to flamenco by a very pissed up Sid, dressed in a Matador costume. He had believed today's events were to celebrate the twinning of Bradford with Bilbao, an industrial seaport with cheap prostitutes. Just like Bilbao. Danny turned and whispered something to Sarah, who immediately left to rescue Maria from Sid's coup de grace. The slaughter of Tony's blind dog, Roy Orbison, with a bronze toasting fork.

Barry appeared from behind the bar with three pints of his best, well moderate, bitter on a tray, gave Danny a firm handshake, fucking hugs, and then opened the previously locked Green Room, beckoning The Three Amigos to enter.

"Come on boys," said Danny, "we've got some work to do."

End

David Coleman's commentary was as crystal clear as ever.

"And the corner is swung in by the diminutive Sunderland winger, Billy Hughes, and the Leeds defence is scrambling. The ball is chested down by Vic Hallam and balls breaks kindly to Ian Porterfield.

One-nil.

Portfield volleys the ball into the roof of the net and the massive underdogs from the second division, Sunderland, have taken the lead in the eighty-ninth minute and surely now must have beaten the mighty Leeds United to win the 1973 FA Cup final.

But wait... There is a linesman's flag up. It looks like an offside and the referee, Ken Burns, has disallowed the goal. The Sunderland team are flocking around the referee to protest but the Leeds keeper Harvey has taken the free kick quickly.

Madeley, the Rolls Royce of all centre backs, drills the ball out wide left to the breaking fullback Trevor Cherry. He feeds it inside to the diminutive Giles, who turns on a sixpence, and then sprays a pinpoint pass to Lorimar on the right. The Sunderland fullback Malone looks very tired now and Lorimar eases past him. He crosses the ball to the far post.

Clarke heads down the cross towards the penalty spot as Mick Jones speeds in and gathers the ball. He beats Dave Watson, then Pitt and fires the ball goalwards. Montgomery dives but his fingertips cannot stop the blistering shot and Leeds take the lead in the ninetieth minute. Surely the cup is theirs now.

The referee looks at his watch, checks with his two linesman and blows the final whistle. Leeds United are the FA Cup champions for the second consecutive year and surely now must be heralded as one of the greatest teams ever, loads better than the Manchester United 1969 European Cup winning side."

The Three Amigos sat back and smiled. Their work was done and they could now get on with the rest of their lives.